DESCENDANTS OF THE BREEDER

PREGNANT WITH FOUR ALPHAS' BABIES
BOOK EIGHT

OLIVIA BHELLE KILDARE
BELLA MOONDRAGON

Copyright © 2024 by Olivia Bhelle Kildare and Bella Moondragon

All rights reserved.

No part of this book may be reproduced in any form or by any electronic or mechanical means, including information storage and retrieval systems, without written permission from the author, except for the use of brief quotations in a book review.

Cover by Sparrow Book Cover Designs

❀ Created with Vellum

CONTENTS

THE ALPHA KINGS' DAUGHTER

Twenty Years Later...
    Trisha

I GROAN as my phone alarm goes off and give it a slap, missing it the first time before my brain finally clears from sleep, and I hit it again before it gets louder. I don't want to wake the whole castle, after all, or anyone in it, really.

I know the guards are always down the hallway, but luckily, it's pretty easy to get around them. Mom and the Dads couldn't keep the hidden tunnels in this place a secret forever, and now that I know about them, they're my best tool when I need to sneak off for an adventure.

And today I really need to get away. Mom has been after me about my birthday coming up—well, all four of our birthdays since we were all born on the same day. But she keeps bothering me about finding out who my mate is like she did with my four dads, and the whole idea is tedious.

There's far too much to explore in this world for the Moon Goddess to hook me up with someone who's going to be overprotective, making me sit in a castle forever, just staring at the world outside through the windows. Life is meant to be lived, and I'm going to live it to the fullest.

The idea of getting away sounds better the more I wake up, so I hurry over to get dressed and grab the bag I'd packed and run a comb through my dark, super curly hair before taking one last look around my room. This time, I plan to be away a bit longer, and honestly, there are a few things I'll miss, like the strange crystal wolf figurine I found last time I explored the castle tunnels. I don't want anyone to take it, so I wrap it up in a towel and hide it behind some books on my bookshelf. Not that anyone would steal from the four Alpha Kings' daughter, but I figure it can't hurt to play it safe.

The tunnel entrance is right outside my room, so I need to get past the guards. They aren't exactly standing right outside my door, but still, it takes some good timing to sneak by quietly and head around the corner where I can take off the wall panel. I've gotten pretty good at putting it back up without it looking like anyone's disturbed it. The tunnel is pretty dark, but I brought my flashlight, though I keep it set on dim so it's not too much of a beacon in case anyone else is down there.

No one ever is.

The place is like a maze, and it's a bit dusty and covered in cobwebs in some places, but I manage to find my way toward the outside entrance, which means I just have a quick sprint before I'm past the side gates. I hate that my wolf hasn't awoken yet because that would make it so much easier, but I've managed to get out on my own dozens of times before.

I remember when my siblings and I were about eight years old. The healer gave us blood tests and told us that we wouldn't get our wolves until we were twenty-one. Apparently, the test to determine that was new at the time. Since everyone gets their wolf at different times, that test has made things easier.

With one more turn before I hit the main exit, I figure I'm in the clear... at least, until I come face-to-face with a brick wall of a man with his arms crossed in front of him.

I sigh. "Dad."

This one is my biological father, Tristan, probably the worst possible person to find me here. I have four dads, which is hard to explain other than my mom has four mates, so they're all my dads. For simplicity's sake, my siblings and I just call them by their first names or just "Dad."

"Trisha."

He doesn't need to say much more. I just march out the side door, the one that leads into the hallway instead of to freedom outside, as he follows me.

"Your mother is waiting for you in the library."

So, he's already told her in the mind-link, and by now, half the castle knows I'm in trouble. There's nothing worse than having one mother and four different fathers all telling you what to do, especially when those four fathers are the Alpha Kings of Dark Forest and the mother is the Luna Queen.

I turn into the library to see Mom sitting on a sofa, and my other dads, Mark, Eli, and Reece, are all standing there with their arms crossed the same way Tristan was before. They're really good at being intimidating, being the Alpha Kings. Mom has told me often of the contest they had before I was born. Back then, she was their breeder, which I can't even wrap my mind around no matter how hard I try. She's always been a Luna Queen to me.

But back then, whoever got her pregnant first was going to be the Alpha King, according to the deal by the old Alpha King, who wasn't even supposed to be on the throne, but Mom ended up pregnant with all four of us—me, my two brothers, and my sister, at the same time, but that's a whole other story.

Over the years, my dads threw the idea of just one king aside and just ruled equally, along with Mom. It works, because everything seems to be running so smoothly… too smoothly, to the point where it's boring here, and I feel the need to get out there. I want to see the world beyond my kingdom and find some people I can help who really need me so I can make a difference in the world, all on my own.

I just need to get out of the castle once in a while to make that happen.

I don't even start to argue with the dads. That's a lost cause. I look straight at my mom, Luna Queen Rose. "Mom, this is ridiculous," I complain. "I'm twenty years old, and there's no reason why I should sit here staring at the walls when there's so much out there for me."

She looks at me sympathetically, which is how she usually looks when I'm trying to tell her that my dads aren't being fair. "I know, sweetie," she says. "We just all worry about you, that's all. All this sneaking around means we don't know where you are or who you're with, and your dads and I worry about that."

"If I tell you I'm going, you all just tell me no," I say. "You've told me so many times that I have what it takes to be a leader, to help people out. Just sitting here in this castle isn't helping anyone."

"Maybe we could send you with an entourage up to the northern territory," Mark suggests. "They need some supplies up there." He looks over at Tristan, who I can't help but notice has that look on his face like there's steam coming out of his ears. "What? I'm just making a suggestion."

"You're not helping, Mark," Tristan says.

I look at Mom, who has her hand over her mouth to hide a smirk. "That could be a good idea, actually," she says. She looks at me. "Sweetie, we just really don't want to ever lose you again."

"Mom," I say calmly. "I was an infant. Yes, a missing baby is cause to panic. I'm twenty—two zero. That's two decades old—and the dads have been training me to defend myself, even without my wolf yet, since I could walk."

Mom looked at Tristan and sighed. "She has a point, dear."

Tristan shakes his head, and his arms are still folded in front of him like a statue that won't budge. And I know he won't. "Little flower, I—" He stops and looks at me. "Trisha, give us a moment, please."

I just shake my head and spin on my heels, walking out of there and straight back to my room. I don't even feel like arguing that I have the right to be there. It's so unfair when it's five against one, well, maybe four against two since Mom sounded like she was being reasonable.

"We're still getting a handle on those rogues," I hear Tristan say as I'm walking down the hall. "Maybe after her birthday, but before that when she doesn't have her wolf, it's too dangerous for her to keep leaving the city alone."

I cover my ears. I don't even want to hear anymore. I've explored the city from top to bottom, and it's out of options for me. Yes, I love the kids at the orphanage, and I don't want to be away from them for long, but I've already gotten that place set up with all the resources it needs. I just have this feeling that there's something out there waiting for me.

I groan as I see two figures approaching—Matthew and Ethan. I'm sure my brothers already know that I was trying to sneak out.

"Trisha, what are you doing?" Ethan asks. "You know we're suppressing an uprising of the rogues. All it takes is to have one of them recognize you, and they'll snatch you up in a second for ransom."

"I'm not going to get snatched," I insist.

"We always recognize you in your disguises," Matthew says.

"You're my brothers," I say. "You see me all day every day. Out there, no one is going to notice me even if I don't wear disguises if I just dress like everyone else."

"But Trisha—"

I wave them off and walk away before Ethan can say another word. It's bad enough having four dads. Having two brothers backing up everything my dads say is unbearable.

I slip into my room and plop on the bed, staring at the ceiling. I recognize a knock on the door, three light taps followed by a heavy one. "Come in."

Reeva peeks her head in first before coming in all the way and shutting the door. "I heard."

I sigh, looking at her. She's got a book in her hand as always. "It's okay. I'll just spend some extra time at the orphanage. Katie drew a picture of me the other day. Maybe I can figure out how to find her a home."

Reeva plopped on the bed beside me. "Please don't keep trying to sneak off," she says. "I'd miss you if I didn't have you to talk to."

"You'd do fine," I insist. "And I'm never gone long. I just need to find someone."

"Is it the dream again?" she asks.

I nod. "I just can't get it out of my mind." I turn to look at her. "Someone's calling me, and I can't tell who. I have to find them, no matter what."

2

ANOTHER ALPHA KING

Damon

"FATHER, I really think you ought to—"

"Nonsense, son!" My father, Alpha King Rohan, bellows from his spot out on the castle balcony. He's very good at bellowing, especially when he's got an idea in his head.

That's never a good thing.

"My spies are going to do a perfect job of infiltrating the Dark Forest realm," he continues. "They'll fit right in. No need to worry about anything, my son. Your daddy has got this."

He smiles the way he always does when he thinks he has a good idea, which unfortunately is all too often. "Thinks" is the operative word. And I know that the idiots he's chosen for the job are going to screw everything up.

"Father, Hans and Brutus don't know the first thing about spying," I say. "Pick someone else from the kingdom—anyone, please."

"Pshaw," he says. He looks at me like he's just seen me for the first time and changes the subject abruptly, as he always does. "My boy, have you found a mate yet?"

I shake my head. "Father, I'll be twenty-one next month."

"Ah, good." He comes up to me and slaps me on the arm. "Well, there's time for that then. Carry on."

He storms by me and runs down the stairs.

I have no idea where he's going other than to get us even deeper into shit, so I just let him run off and stroll out onto the balcony myself. I see the team of idiots loading useless garbage onto the vehicles that will soon be bound for the docks.

I shake my head, looking around. From the high perch, I can see the entire city and far off into the distance, where the billowing clouds meet the snow-covered mountains that border the inland pass. It's not possible to see all of our Green Mountain realm, but I can admire all the progress we've made in modernization, mostly in spite of my father.

Looking in the other direction, I can see the ocean, and across the wide blue expanse lies our enemies, the Alphas of the Dark Forest realm. It's hard to imagine what's over there on the other side of those unfriendly waves, and whether they're readying ships to come attack us or minding their own business is anyone's guess.

But wondering isn't enough for my father. He's been obsessed with the other realm since the day my mother passed away. She was his true mate, and most of his soul seems to have died with her. At first, he screamed for nights on end, shifting and running off into the woods. The guards would report to me what they'd found the next day, and the sight was never pleasant.

But it was even worse when he stopped screaming and grew quiet, sinking into himself and developing a whole world within his mind that did not match the world around him.

It was then that his obsession began with the Dark Forest realm. Somehow, it's their fault that my mother was taken from us. His downward spiral has increased until he lost all the wisdom he'd ever had and became a shell of a man. Where once he was brilliant, now he's a bumbling idiot just like Hans and Brutus.

I guess it's his way of bottoming out.

"Red wine! Why the hell don't we have any red wine to go with the venison!"

I close my eyes as if that will drown him out as he screams at the cook downstairs. It won't.

"Incompetent fools! We're celebrating our newest accomplishment!"

I gaze at the "accomplishment" as they give each other a swift high-five and pile into the backseat with stacks of baggage strapped onto a trailer behind them.

"I'm pretty sure that spies travel light." Having no one to hear me, I turn around and go back to my suite in the heart of the castle, imagining the end game in the war my father is instigating with his idiocy.

I ARRIVE at the campus early the next morning. I always hate leaving Father alone—Goddess knows what stupid decision he'll make next—but I have a responsibility to fulfill in my training.

The university is larger than most cities in my realm but for good reason. It houses not only the best programs in every subject imaginable, but it also has the Alpha training program for every pack in the realm. Though my future position as Alpha King is different from everyone else's and requires special training at the castle, I still show up on campus as often as I can. Getting to know the other Alphas in the realm is an important part of my future, one that I take very seriously.

"Future Alpha King Damon." Alpha Axel approaches me and offers his hand, which I shake. He's in his late thirties, a well-tested warrior with the respect of everyone in the program.

"I do wish you'd call me Damon and not all those titles, Alpha Axel."

His amber eyes twinkle as he laughs. "I doubt your father would approve."

"My father approves of nothing but battling Dark Forest warriors on the other side of the ocean," I say sadly.

He nods. "The kingdom sorely misses our Luna Queen. I take it the Alpha King hasn't given up his quest to begin a war?"

"No." I sigh. "So, we need to keep all our warriors in top shape for the mess he's starting. I can't stop him, Axel."

He puts a hand on my shoulder. "There is no healing a lost mate."

"And that's why I'll never go there," I say.

"Aye, but the realm will need a Luna Queen once you take the throne," he says. "And you'll need an heir. Don't give up hope for that. Not all mate bonds are tragic. Look at my parents. Sixty years together and still in wedded bliss."

I shake my head, and he snickers. "Well, Future Alpha King Damon, my students are waiting for me. I take it you're here for the warrior training?"

"Yes. It's as good a way as any to assess the leaders of the other packs."

He nods. "Don't be too rough on them." He laughs as he walks away, and I give him the finger.

"Now, is that any way for a future Alpha King to behave?" A familiar voice has me spinning around.

"Braden. Are they still letting the likes of you on campus?" I give him my best scowl, and he approaches with a fake bow.

"Alpha King, I beg your forgiveness, my great Alpha King, but none can be as great as you," he says.

"Jackass." We both laugh, and I hit him on the arm.

"Just keeping you on your toes," he says. "Where's Alessandro?"

"Gone for a few weeks. I sent him ahead of those other clowns to Dark Forest," I explain.

"Oh, a real spy." He laughs again, but I feel a headache coming on thinking of my father's ideas.

"Well, Father forced my hand," I say. "It's either see what's going on for myself or get stuck trusting Hans Fralig."

He raises an eyebrow. "Yeah... no. That dude'll do anything for a pile of gems."

"Don't remind me."

He tries not to laugh as we head toward the training grounds. "The Starlight pack boys are here."

It was my turn to raise an eyebrow. "Oh? They're never on campus. Good. It'll give me a chance to check them out. Father thinks they're great, which means I can't trust them to throw a stick."

"I wouldn't give them the stick to throw in the first place," he says. "They'll as soon poke your eye out with it."

"I'd like to see them try."

He laughs. "Oh, I'd pay money to see you shift and tear them apart."

"But I won't for now. Till we work on better relationships with those northern packs. I don't want to see the ore up there go to waste. We can't get trade treaties by tearing up all their Alphas."

"You're right," he agrees. "But it would still be fun. So, have you been seeing that Alisa girl again?"

"Who?"

"Alisa, the redhead with the big… you know," he says.

"You really need to stop thinking with what's in your pants," I say as he shrugs. "And I've never seen her to begin with. What makes you think I have?"

"She's bragging to all her friends that she's bagged the future Alpha King," he explains.

"Bagged me? If I've ever touched her, it was because she bumped into me in a crowd." I frown at him. I have to be a little more selective as a future Alpha King, so I don't let just any woman close to me. If I have a choice, I'd rather forget the whole mating and heir thing altogether. But since I can't for the sake of my kingdom, I need to at least stay away from the hussies. Braden, on the other hand, likes to play the field. I guess it's easy when you only have your own pack to worry about.

"Well, you'd better set her straight," he says.

"Eh, it doesn't matter," I say. "If the whole kingdom thinks I'm taken, at least they'll leave me alone."

He laughs. "My man, you're not going to get an heir that way. You know, that old Alpha King in Dark Forest held a contest with a breeder. Turns out that one woman ended up having heirs for all four of the winning contestants at once."

"Yeah, I know," I say. "They're all four the Alpha Kings now I hear, and they made her Luna Queen. Can you believe it? A breeder as the Luna Queen."

He shrugs. "I don't know. I heard she's nice."

I look at him and shake my head. "What does that have to do with anything?"

"Well, a nice lady as Luna Queen—we could use that here, don't you think?" He wiggles his eyebrows, and I just glare at him.

"I suppose a breeder could be my Luna Queen if she just leaves me alone except for when I need her."

He laughs. "Well, that'll win you points with her. You want to be kind to your mate."

"I don't need points, and I don't need to be kind," I say. "I need to run a kingdom. Now, let's get to the training grounds."

I turn, and he follows me. I feel a pounding sensation in my gut. But I ignore it.

The last thing I need is a mate.

3

LAUNCHING AN ADVENTURE

Trisha

I've been staring at the ceiling for half the night, gazing at the rays of moonlight that slip through the curtain dancing on the ceiling. I don't have my wolf yet, but I feel like she's already restless.

I understand my mom's point of view. I've heard a thousand times about the kidnapping when I was a baby, how some crazy woman snuck away with me and how they were lucky to find me.

I don't want to scare her again, but this is different. I just don't feel like I belong here, not right now, and something about that moonlight is tugging on my heartstrings, begging me to leave the castle.

My sister doesn't want me to go, but she seems to at least understand that I'm hearing some sort of calling from somewhere far away. Every time I drift off to sleep, I see him in my dreams. It's strange because he always looks like someone different, or at least, there's been three different versions of him that I've counted so far.

Sometimes, he asks for my help. Other nights, he's just there, and something in my heart pulls me toward him as if I'm lost until I find him. Every time I leave the castle, I try to close my eyes and feel him in my heart until I can feel his direction.

But then, I always get caught.

My brothers and my dads—they'll never understand me, and I've given up trying. I know they mean well. But my mother went far away from her home, and that was where she found them, and look at how their lives all changed.

Reeva seems to think that it's my mate in my dream, but I don't think so. The idea of a mate just sounds so repulsive—always having someone demanding to know where you were. I get enough of that from my family.

I just have the feeling that it's someone calling to me for help from far away.

I sit up, throwing off my covers and running into my bathroom to change. I grab my bag, which is still packed and in my closet, and this time, I grab the wolf statue that I'd hidden before and throw it in.

It's later in the night than I usually leave, which seems to be an advantage because the guard looks like he's drifting off. I open my door a bit wider than the small crack I'd used to scout out the hallway and slip out, not even breathing until I'm in down the hall in the library that has the other passageway entrance.

I use the knob to open it up and slip in, stopping to listen for several minutes to be sure one of my dads isn't standing guard. I guess they figure I wouldn't try again so soon because the coast is clear, and I slip out the back of the castle wall at a point where it's only a quick sprint to the forest. In seconds I'm there, clear of the castle but still quiet and cautious so I don't get caught this time.

There's just one more obstacle—the city walls, which are heavily guarded. People come and go at all hours of the night, so there are plenty of guards on different shifts. There's no chance of finding them asleep and sneaking by. I'm going to have to bribe them.

I duck into an alleyway near the entrance and dig through my bag. For a second, my hand hits the wolf statue, and I consider using that. I pull it out, looking at it and noticing for the first time that it has some type of carvings on it in the moonlight. I decide not to let go of it until I know what those are for sure. It might be worth more money than I'd need to bargain my way out of Dark Forest City.

Putting it back in my pack, I reach for my gold, grab a few coins, and head for the gate. I take one last deep breath before passing through.

"Miss."

I wince, having almost made it by before the guard called me back.

"Yes?" I say without turning around.

He walks over in front of me.

Great.

"You look a bit young to be off at night," he says. "It's dangerous out there. Do your parents know where you are?"

Happy that he hasn't recognized me, I paste on my innocent face. It's lucky that I didn't wear anything that looked royal, though I rarely do anyway.

"I need to pick up some medicine from my aunt in Belshire," I say. "Mom is sick and the pharmacies in town are out."

He looks at me for a while as if measuring my honesty, so I do my best to read 'innocent girl' in my eyes.

"Belshire's awfully far to walk," he says.

"I-I'm going to shift and run," I explain. I figure that since I'm almost old enough to shift, I probably look the part.

He nods but just keeps standing there, not saying anything but not letting me leave either. I narrow my eyes.

Greedy bastard.

"Oh," I say, still feigning innocence. "Is there a toll for the gate? Here." I hand him the gold. "Is this enough?"

"It'll do," he says, putting it in his pocket. He steps back, and I turn around and walk forward, trying not to break into a run.

Once clear of the gate I step into the forest, leaning against a tree and taking off my shoes to feel the soul of the forest in me. For some reason, I'm more in touch with things that way and feel like I can find whoever it is I'm looking for.

A vision of the docks comes to mind. I shiver a little, and not because I'm cold. Ships run up and down the coast all the time. I'm not afraid of that. But some ships go over the ocean to a whole other realm.

If the man calling for me is way over there, I'll be a long way from home.

ETHAN

"DAD, I can't go running off on some assignment when Trisha is missing," I say.

The whole house is in upheaval, and it's barely 5:00 in the morning. I hate the look of worry in Mom's eyes and just want to be part of the search crew. She can't be far.

"We have a whole castle full of people looking for your sister," he assures me.

Alpha Eli, my biological father, does not look any calmer than my mother. I know he's right, that there are whole armies of warriors who can search for Trisha, but I just need to feel like I'm doing something to help.

"Unfortunately, this is an emergency assignment that can't wait," he says. "We always find your sister, and she's never far. But we have a problem up to the north at the resort."

I've heard the story of that place many times, where my father and aunt were trapped for a few days with some rogues who had taken over an abandoned resort deep in the forest. Their leader was apparently insane from the loss of his mate, and the people were nearly starving.

Dad didn't abandon them, though. As soon as he could, he sent a team to fix up the place and make them all members of our pack.

"Your aunt Kelly sent a distress call yesterday," he continues. "She wouldn't send that unless she really needed the help. I've had a contingent of warriors getting ready all night, and I need you to lead them."

I sigh. I'd met Aunt Kelly only a few times, but she always acted like she'd known me forever. Ever since I could remember she's lived at the resort with her mate, running things and reporting back to my dad. There haven't been any problems until now.

"It's at the very edge of the territory," he says. "That far out, the Stone pack, led by Alpha Drake, has a long history of questioning the authority of the Alpha Kings, back long before King Gene and even his father's reign. If they're causing trouble now, that could mean war if we can't get a handle on this now."

I take in a breath. I understand the importance of maintaining the crown's power. If every pack just did whatever they wanted to, there would be nothing but war in the whole realm, which I understand was the way it used to be when King Gene was in charge.

I need to go to keep things peaceful in our realm. That, and I need to protect my aunt if she's in danger. She's a really nice person who seems to care about others quite a bit.

I nod. "I'll be at the front gate in thirty minutes," I say.

"Make it twenty," Dad replies.

I nod again and make my way back to my suite at a fast pace. I have to stop halfway there, though, as the former Alpha King and Queen are taking a stroll down the hallway, and I have to give them a quick bow.

Former Alpha King Edward nods and Former Luna Queen Marcella gives a slight curtsy. The couple is getting very old but always looks so happy. I've grown up in the castle with them around, and they always seem to have time for children, to tell a story or look at something we'd made.

Theirs was a terrible story. The former Alpha King Gene, their son, had stolen the crown from them and kept them prisoner separately to keep their minds foggy. They are true mates selected by the Moon Goddess herself; that is clear in the way they look at each other.

But for my entire life they have both been free, enjoying life in the castle with no responsibilities. Though King Gene had no right to assign the throne to anyone, King Edward has accepted my dads' rule.

In fact, he has encouraged it, especially since they had rescued and reunited him with his mate.

Once I pass them, I head down the hall and into my room, quickly assessing what things I need to bring, knowing that the warriors likely have all the provisions necessary even if we need to fight a battle.

I'm a few months away from getting my wolf, so I will take a back seat to those warriors while still guiding them on. All four of my Alpha dads have trained me in combat strategy from an early age.

Satisfied that I have everything I need in the bag and still worrying about Trisha, I head toward the front gate.

4

WHICH SHIP?

Ethan

My unofficial aunt and uncle, Shelby and Sam, are riding with me in the SUV on the journey to the resort. Sam was once Beta for the corrupt Alpha King Gene, though Sam has always been an honorable man that I count as family.

I'm not crazy about having my aunt in harm's way, but there's no stopping her from coming to see my biological aunt Kelly, mostly because Kelly's daughter is pregnant, and they haven't seen them in so long.

Her son, Isaac, is set to be the Alpha in this territory once we handle the problems here. Apparently, descendants of the original rogues who took over when the place was abandoned think they can waltz in and claim it as their territory.

Not with my four fathers in charge.

A tall man greets us on the outskirts, his hair the same shade of red as mine. He waits as our driver parks and meets me at the door almost before I have a chance to step out.

"I'd know that hair anywhere," he says with a laugh, holding out his arm amiably. "Cousin, it's good to see you again. It's been a long time."

I shake his hand firmly. "Why we don't see each other more often, I have no idea. It's good to see you, although I wish it was under better circumstances."

"As do I," he says, nodding. "I hate to bother the Alpha Kings' army, but I thought it best that we don't let these rogues think they can encroach on the crown's land."

"That's true," I agree.

"Oh, where are my manners? I've never introduced you to my future Beta, Katherine—" He nodded toward the woman at his side with short dark hair. "And you probably remember my father's Beta, Andrew."

"Good to meet you, and good to see you again," I say. I haven't seen a pack with a female Beta before, but this woman seems certainly capable, her physique powerful and her stance confident. She nods lightly, just once, at her introduction, and I return the gesture.

"Well, let's get back to the compound," Isaac says. "We've had a good day without any attacks so far, so we won't need to get to skirmishing with rogues tonight."

"My warriors will be disappointed," I say.

He laughs and pats me on the back. "Your warriors and I will get along well. Come, we have a dinner prepared for you."

"You didn't need to go to any trouble," I said. "I have a lot of warriors to feed and plenty of rations. I could dine with them."

"My mother will kill me if I don't feed you." He laughed. "She's waiting as well, along with my sister, so let's head in."

I instruct the warriors to follow, and we make our way toward the resort compound where the army sets up camp on the outskirts while I head over to the resort. It's impressive, with well-manicured grounds and several buildings and outbuildings that are all in pristine shape.

I see the clone of my hair again as a woman approaches us, holding her belly. "Ethan!" My cousin Isabelle pulls me in for a hug, which is difficult to navigate with her advanced pregnancy.

"Hmm, you look pretty far along seeing as how your mother just told me about this."

We both pull out of the hug to see Shelby tapping her foot with mock anger in her expression.

"I'm so sorry, Shelby," Isabelle says, giving her a hug.

Kelly walks up behind her and starts explaining. "We keep meaning to head back to the castle again, but something always comes up. I know I should get a message to you since we're out of mind-link range. It's been so much work out here, and so many people need me—"

"Kelly, stop explaining," Shelby says with a laugh. "Though you could send a messenger once in a while. We just miss you, that's all." She moves in and gives her a gentle hug. "I'd better see my niece's little one more often than I've seen Isaac and Isabelle over the years."

"You will, I promise," Isabelle says.

Kelly smiles. "Come on, let's get inside. We've made Sam's favorite."

"Anything that's food is my favorite," Sam jokes.

We all laugh as we make our way into a large, open living space with multiple levels. As we enter, my attention turns to a woman about my age with long, dark, curly hair that sweeps over her shoulders like silk. She walks up to Katherine and takes her weapon from her, saying a few quiet words before moving on.

As she passes me on her way out, I lock eyes with her for a split second, her deep blue irises surrounded by flecks of silver.

Trisha

I take a deep breath when I get to the docks. It's just before sunrise, and the place is already crawling with fishermen getting ready for a day's work and sailors loading their vessels to travel either up the coast or across the ocean to the one place I'd never visited, the enemy realm.

I need to figure out where my calling is leading me. I've been up all night with no time for dreams, so I've relied on my forest sense to tell me which way to go. I'm not surprised that it led me to the docks. I know now that this is going to be quite an adventure.

But now… which ship?

It's clear that I'm not to go with the fishermen, and frankly I'm glad, so I must be destined for a sailing voyage. Since the Moon Goddess has led me this far, I'm sure that whatever ship I get on will be the right one. But I'm still not sure how to choose.

There's a white ship that catches my eye. It's a little bigger than the others, and they're loading some heavy crates on board. It looks a bit cleaner than all the others, so I decide to go with that one.

I tie my hair back into a ponytail and take another breath, double checking my clothes to be sure they look a little worn out so I'll blend in. People aren't exactly dressed as royalty here.

That's what makes it so great.

I head directly toward the white ship, figuring that if I look like I know what I'm doing, no one will ask questions. Of course, there aren't many women around here, so I sort of stick out like a sore thumb anyway, but I'll never get anywhere if I don't just go for it.

I make it down to the docks and I'm halfway up the pier toward the white ship when I almost trip over a sailor untying a rope.

"Best hurry, miss," he says. "We're needin' to make quick time."

"Who, me?" I ask.

"Yer the lassie who bought the passage, ain't ya?" he asks back.

I look around, seeing no other woman standing anywhere around. I look at the man for a moment. He's very thin, like his last meal was a few days ago, yet he seems to have an air of energy that I see in our kingdom's best warriors.

I look up at the ship he's unmooring. It's about half the size of the white one and dirty as a pair of socks on my brothers' bedroom floor. There's something about it that looks strong, though, like it's been on a thousand voyages and can't wait for a thousand more.

"Well, ain't ya?" he repeats.

Taking one last look at the white ship, I realize I'm going to have a hard time explaining why I'm there. But I actually I have a free ride right in front of me.

Time to take a chance.

"Yes, I am," I say. "I'm sorry I took so long."

"Well, get aboard 'er and let's get goin'," he says.

I don't waste any time climbing up the somewhat rickety plank, sticking next to the sailor so he can vouch for me when people start asking questions. That happens fast.

"Hey, no girlie friends," a stern man tells him almost as soon as I'm on the ship.

"Ain't no girlie friend," the skinny sailor says. "This be the gal who booked passage."

"Oh," the other man says. He looks me up and down. "Apologies, miss. You must be Daphne. Your father wants me to look after you, so I've arranged a room away from all these dirty seabies. Follow me."

I nod, neither confirming nor denying the name of Daphne, and follow this man, who seems to be well fed and better dressed than any of the others.

I find out why soon enough.

"Cap'n," a man greets him as we descend to the lower deck.

The captain stops the man as he's walking by. "This here's Daphne, Roland's daughter. Watch out for her, and let the others know to leave her be, understood?"

"Aye, aye, Cap'n," the man says, walking on.

The captain leads me to a room, and suddenly I'm alone, dropping my tired body and my bag on the cot. It's small but private, and at least I'm finally going somewhere. I lie back, exhausted, and drift off to sleep.

"Hey."

I blink my eyes awake more from the smell of bad breath in my face than from the stranger's voice. My vision is blurred at first but quickly comes into focus on the man from the hallway the night before.

"Daphne, right?" he says.

I nod, thankful that I'm with it enough to remember my fake name. I'm glad I'm still fully dressed since he barged in like that. "Yes. What time is it?"

"Supper," he says.

"I slept all day?"

"Lucky you," he says with a smirk. "Most o'the crew has to work for a livin'. Best get to the mess hall if you wanna eat."

I nod again, getting up and throwing on a sweater and stashing my bag in the little cabinet by the cot. I follow him down a few hallways that look exactly the same. We're still below deck, but I catch a glimpse of the open sea in the window.

There's no going back now.

"I'm Randy," he says.

"Happy to meet you, Randy." I smile at him when he takes a second to turn around.

"Oh, you will be, Daphne. Don't worry. You'll be very happy with me." He lets out a snarling laugh that sends goosebumps up my arms at his joke.

At least, I hope it's a joke.

5

MAGNETISM

Ethan

Isaac and his future Beta, Katherine, join me and my future Beta, Cameron, for a meeting the next morning.

Isaac lays out a map on the conference room table. "Most of our trouble is from the north. But they do have a tendency to sneak around the east side and try to breach the guard line there. It's never been a huge battle, but all these little skirmishes are wearing a hole in our defenses. We need to put a stop to it."

I nod. "Well, we'll give them the show of force they're looking for," I say. "I have enough warriors to reinforce both sides."

"Last night, I caught a whiff of rogue scent on the western flank."

I look up. It's the first time Katherine has said a word, but until now, she hasn't needed to, I suppose. It's good intel, and I appreciate it. I nod toward her. "Then we'll need a full perimeter, at least until we get enough intel to break past our territory and get them where they're hiding."

The scent of chocolate mint wafts by me, and I forget my next sentence and pause for a second. Cameron looks at me with a raised brow, but I get my bearings quickly.

"Let's break into teams for the day and send some scouts out," I say.

"Good thing the Alpha Kings' men have come to save us." The tone is sarcastic, but the voice sounds like the finest violin, its music warm and deep, penetrating my soul.

I look up to see the raven-haired beauty I'd seen yesterday, her silver flecked eyes glaring straight at me.

Kathleen speaks up. "Alpha King Heir, please forgive my sister, Rylee. She's a bit sour about all things royal."

Instantly, I know that Rylee's smirk will haunt my dreams tonight.

TRISHA

I'VE BEEN on the ship for over three weeks now, and I'm starting to get used to the food, which is bland but fills me up at least. I'm also starting to get the hang of the way the waves have me constantly moving. It wasn't something I'd considered before I hopped aboard, but if it's part of the journey I have to take, I'll deal with it.

I'm not the only woman on board, but I might as well be to all these sailors since the nice blonde named Hilda is mated to Carlile, one of the biggest and scariest guys on the ship. I like Hilda, and we've been having fun talking a lot. It's sort of like having a sister on the ship. But since she's off-limits to the crew, all the other guys spend way too much time staring at me, sometimes directly and other times trying to sneak a look while I'm walking past. I always catch them at it.

None have been worse than Randy, who was fairly aptly named, apparently, being an awfully *randy* guy. He's taken it on himself to escort me everywhere I need to go, which I suppose could be considered polite, but the way I catch him ogling me constantly gives me the creeps. I've just been ignoring him and spending most of my time with Hilda when I can.

Tonight, I'm lying on my cot, all settled in to re-read one of the two books I packed. I hadn't exactly been planning for downtime, but luckily, they're good books. I'm just getting to the good part as the gentle rocking of the ship starts to lull me to sleep.

But then my door rattles, and I come to attention. Randy opens the door, which I know I've locked, with a sick grin on his face. I pull my sheet up over me and scoot back toward the wall.

"Oh, now, is that any way to greet me?" he asks, his grin widening and causing a chill in me. "I've seen the way you've been lookin' at me, lass. Let's stop playing here."

I sit up straight and frown, answering in my harshest voice. "What are you doing in here? I locked the door for a reason."

"Ah, lassie, now we both know that ain't true," he says. "You knew I had the key."

"I did not!" I glance sideways, but my bag is on the other side of the cabin so I can't grab my knife, the only weapon I have with me. Goddess, I wish I could shift already.

"Just relax," he says. "Whoever y'had before, he won't stand up to my skills." He eyes me carefully, and I feel like I want to throw up. "Ah, so y'haven't had a man before. This will be more fun than I thought."

"Nothing's going to be any fun," I say firmly. "Get out of my room!"

He just laughs and takes a step toward me. The last thing I want is for him to tackle me in bed, so I stand up and instantly regret it, my pajama shorts set revealing a bit more than I want to without a bra.

He practically drools, and I feel like throwing up again.

"Get out," I repeat.

"Not till I'm finished," he says. "And this will take a while. I'm well known for being very good at this. Don't worry, though, lassie. You'll like it soon. I won't be rough… or at least, not too rough."

"I said get out." Having two brothers and living in the castle with top warrior self-defense training has its advantages. The guy is old enough to shift, so I know I'm in trouble if he tries that, but I'm a pretty good fighter regardless. I move into my fighting stance, one that always manages to take down my brothers.

He just laughs again and steps closer. "Come on, now. I'll have you purring like a kitten in no time. You'll be my little kitten for the rest o' the trip."

"I'll be nothing of the sort," I said. "Get out. I'm warning you."

"You're warning me? Oh, that's a laugh." He closes the distance between us and reaches out to slap me, but I duck quickly and spin around.

In an instant he grabs for my neck and whirls around me till he has me in a chokehold. I smile. This is one of my best moves. I grab his hand and duck under his arm, slipping out of his hold and twisting his arm in the process, but I don't finish the move because he kicks backward at me and trips me. I fall down on the floor.

He smiles down at me in a disgusting way, and I reach up to kick him in another good move just as the door flies off its hinges and sails across the room.

In an instant, Randy's off his feet, slammed up against the wall by a big, muscular arm. It's an outside wall, so I look at it, worried whoever it is might ram Randy straight through it and sink the whole ship.

"She said get out," says a low, gravelly voice.

Randy has his arms up in surrender, and I'm afraid he's going to pee right on my floor. Between that and no door, I'm definitely going to need to change rooms.

"I'm going, I'm going," he says.

Muscle man lets go of him, and Randy runs faster than I ever thought he was capable of. I'm still standing here with my mouth half open in shock about whatever that was, and I turn to face the new man in my room.

Looking at the guy full-on, I have to force myself to close my mouth and not just sit there and drool. He's tall, blond, and every inch of the man is just as muscular as his arm. I have to blink twice because I'm sure I'm seeing things, but his eyes are actually silver.

"Are you okay?" he asks.

I stand here for a minute trying to figure out how to answer that. I look down at my pajamas, which are still intact but strewn a little sideways and way more revealing than they're supposed to be. I look back up at the man as I feel heat rising in my cheeks, and in other places, throwing me off-kilter a bit. I've almost forgotten who I am and how much I hate being treated like a damsel in distress. If this were anyone else, I would yell at the guy. But somehow, I'm barely capable of saying anything.

"I'm fine," I say finally. "I had that handled."

"I'm sure you did," he says. "Still, Randy needs to be shown who's boss once in a while."

"And I suppose you're the boss?" I don't know why I said that or what that even means. I can't even talk straight around this guy.

He chuckles, and it sounds like music. "Only when the right people need a proper lesson. Roland and I go way back. I'm just trying to pay him back for a favor. Didn't mean to step on toes."

"I—" I have no idea how to respond to that, then I remember who I'm supposed to be—Daphne, Roland's daughter. That's right. "Well, thanks then. You can consider him repaid, um—"

"Alessandro." He holds out his hand, and I just stare at it. Goddess, even the man's name is sexy. I shake my head to snap out of it and take his hand.

"Good to meet you, Alessandro," I say, giving him a firm handshake and not letting go quite soon enough. I blush again and look over at my empty doorway.

"Oh, sorry for that," he says. "I'll switch rooms with you. I'm down at the other end of the hall. I don't need a door."

I wonder for a moment why this guy has his own room, but then I look at him and lose track of all my thoughts.

What's wrong with me?

"I guess I'll take you up on that, then," I say. "I could use some sleep."

"Randy definitely doesn't have a key to my door, so he won't be bothering you again," he says.

I nod, realizing I've been staring at his bicep. "Oh, good. Well, I'll just… get my bag here. Are you sure taking your room is okay?"

"Of course it is," he insists. "I broke your door, after all."

I nod, timidly walking by him to grab my bag and leave, catching my breath as I head down to the other room. I don't even care that I'm walking down the hall in my skimpy pajamas. I normally like to take care of problems myself, but I can't say I'm going to argue if this man breaks down my door and rescues me again.

Trisha, what are you saying?

After I finally get settled in the room that smells amazingly like Alessandro, it takes a long time to get to sleep.

I don't think I'm out for a whole hour when I hear hollering on the ship and open my eyes to see that it's dawn. "Land ho!"

6

—————

A WHOLE NEW REALM

Trisha

I'M NOT sure what I expected. After years of being told Green Mountain is horrible, and the people there are primitive, I'm shocked to pull into the docks that look almost identical to the ones I left weeks ago. At least maritime-wise, everything here seems to be the same.

That includes creepy sailors. I hold my bag close while disembarking, and just about every one of the guys on the ship "accidentally" bumps into me, and it only gets worse when I hit the docks with hundreds of other sailors hanging around.

I catch a quick glimpse of Alessandro, but he quickly disappears around a corner toward the town. I look around, not really sure which way to go. I'm surrounded by a huge, busy metropolis without a forest to be seen anywhere, so there's clearly not going to be a way to get in touch with whatever force is guiding me here.

The best I can do is pick a direction and go, so I choose the way that Alessandro headed. His scent seems to be still alive in my mind,

31

and I'm not sure why. I don't usually even notice a guy's scent unless it's rancid, which happens more often than I'd like.

The further I get into the heart of the city, the more other women are around me, so it's a huge relief. I decide to explore the city a bit before I find somewhere to stay for the night, so I just keep strolling around, looking in all the shop windows. Though I find more than a few things I'd love to buy, holding onto my money is a bit more important right now since I'm not sure how long I'll be here.

I spot a little boy crying on the corner.

"What's wrong?" I ask, walking up to him. "Are you lost?"

He nods, tears still streaming down his cheeks. He's really adorable, and I feel awful. I stand up and look around, but no one seems to be looking for him.

"What's your name?" I ask.

"Kenny."

"Well, Kenny, I'm… I'm Daphne." I decide to stick to my fake name in case anyone from the ship is still around me.

"That's a pretty name," he says through his tears.

"Thanks. Let's find your mommy, okay?"

He nods, and I take his hand and walk to where there are a few more people. After a few minutes, I see panicked eyes in the crowd.

"Ma'am!" I call to the woman. "Is this your boy over here?"

"Oh, thank the Goddess!" The woman runs over to us and picks up Kenny in a tight hug. "Thank you so much," she says to me.

"No problem at all," I say. "I'm glad he's safe with you."

Smiling at how cute the boy is, I keep walking to explore the city. I'm not sure how it happens, but time gets away from me, and the sun is already starting to set. I look around and have no idea where I'm at. The shops seem to end on this street, and there's nothing but houses to follow, so I turn around and head back, hoping to find a hotel somewhere in the middle of the shopping district.

But there's nothing…. All around me are stores that are starting to shutter for the night, and the street is starting to empty out.

"Okay, let's figure this out," I say to myself.

I look up and down the street, and it's hard to recognize where

I've been now that the shopkeepers have pulled in the displays that were out on the sidewalks. With no obvious hotels in this area, I turn on a side street that looks like it's still part of the business district, but that soon turns into houses as well.

Another street looks promising, but it turns out to be a dead end. I sigh and stop for a moment to get my bearings, but then I catch a whiff of a scent... and it grows into three more scents. I take a deep breath and turn around.

And there they stand, four fairly burly guys with big shitty grins on their faces like cats who just cornered a mouse. I curse silently that I can't shift yet because these guys definitely can, judging by their ages.

It isn't like I've never been through a similar situation before, though. Since I can't use my wolf, a little smooth talking usually gets me through, and if not, I'm a pretty good fighter even in human form.

I spend a few seconds sizing these guys up to figure out what might convince them. They're no sailors, which might be good because there's only one thing those guys want, and that means a tough fight. They're most likely thieves, which is good in some ways because I might outsmart them but bad in others since I don't have much money to give up and need every coin I'm currently carrying.

"Hey, guys," I say when I finally make up my mind. "It looks like I'm a little turned around. Could you point me toward the Alpha's mansion? He's expecting me." I figure if they think I know the Alpha of these parts they might be less likely to mess with me.

It doesn't work.

Instead, they laugh. The tall one who I could probably take on my own if he didn't have backup, moves in closer. "Oh, yeah? What's the Alpha's name?"

Shoot. I wasn't expecting that. I rack my brain trying to remember some of the so-called enemy Alphas my dads had talked about from Green Mountain, but all I can think of is one.

"Alpha Rohan," I say. I hope that's a good choice.

Apparently, it isn't, because they start laughing harder. Skinny guy speaks up again. "Alpha King Rohan?"

Oh, damn. Bad choice.

He gets up so close I can smell his bad breath. "Sweetie, you're nowhere near the castle, and what would the Alpha King want with the likes of you? I think you're lying to us. What do you think, boys?"

"Yeah, the broad is lyin'."

I don't know which guy says that because I'm not taking my eyes off the tall one since he's completely in my personal space. In fact, I have to back up a couple of steps to get away from the guy, but he just keeps moving forward. I realize instantly that I've made a mistake because now he has me up against the wall.

I start assessing which spot to hit first. I'm pretty sure I can immobilize him, but then I'd need to get through his posse. They don't seem smart, but they're all pretty big.

"I'm not lying." I decide to stick with my story. "Alpha King Rohan is expecting me. I'm the daughter of one of his friends in the north." Now I know I'm really getting deep in it because I have no idea what the geography of this kingdom is like. I really wish I'd paid attention in class when they taught this stuff, but now that I'm here, it seems like my teachers didn't have the right information about this place, either.

He's laughing again, and that can't be good. "Oh, you keep digging yourself a deeper hole. Where have you been living, in an eastern cave? Ain't nothin' up north but snow and ice."

I wince a little inside but try to hide it. I'm starting to realize that fighting my way out of this is the only way to go. I just have to figure out how to get around those bulldogs he's got behind him. I think about yelling for help just to get some backup, but around here as dark as it's starting to get, I'll probably just have more guys to fight off.

I'm just about to make my move to take down the tall guy when I catch a whiff of one of the most wonderful scents I'd ever smelled, so good it overpowers this guy's bad breath. It confuses me a little bit, and I hold off my attack. It seems to be a mix of strawberries and green apples, two of my favorite fruits. I hadn't noticed a scent this strong since Alessandro.

What's wrong with me?

"What's going on back here?" The voice is definitely all Alpha... stronger than that, really. It leaves the tall guy trembling, and he immediately backs away from me.

"We were just... helping this young lady find her way," he whimpers.

"Yeah. We was just givin' directions." Big guy number two has a stupid grin on his face while he says it.

"Get out." The power the Alpha says it with even makes me want to high-tail it out of there, but I stand my ground, still feeling a bit woozy from that scent. The four guys harassing me are gone in an instant, and the Alpha guy approaches me.

Now that I can see him in the light, I swallow, trying to clear the lump out of my throat. My heart's beating so hard I can hear it in my chest, and I know he can, too.

Now, I know for sure something's wrong with me. I like to look at eye candy like any other woman, but usually I don't freeze up and act like a babbling idiot around anybody. I figure being in a different kingdom is having an effect on me. Maybe there's some magic here that makes people a little fuzzy in the head.

He gets close, really close, but somehow I don't even care that this hunk of a man is in my personal space. I can see him a little better as he steps more into the streetlight. His jet black hair is the same color as mine but straight, not curly. His eyes are the color of the ocean, not the one I just crossed, but like the one just off the coast where people go for a beach vacation.

"Are you all right, miss?"

I'm starting to like his voice just a little too much. I see another man walk up behind him, keeping his distance yet keeping watch. It has to be his Beta. The presence of someone else snaps me out of whatever stupor I was in. I'm not even sure what that was, but I feel like myself again.

"I'm fine," I say. "And I had that handled."

The Alpha's eyes go a little wide. "Oh, you did, huh? Well, sorry to intrude, miss."

"I'm just trying to find a hotel to stay in," I say a little louder than I mean to.

"Ah, well, this is a bad neighborhood for that," he says. "Let us show you back to the right street for that. I'm Alpha Heir Damon, and this is my future Beta, Daniel."

Alpha Heir....

So, this is Alpha King Rohan's son. I give him a polite nod though I'm still feeling frazzled. For the second time in as many days, some big burly dude—sexy as they may be—have burst into my life and pretended to save me from something I could have handled on my own.

If I wanted to be protected, I could have just hung out at home at the castle. I guess this is my life now.

At least they know where the hotels are. I shrug and follow them, trying to ignore those strawberries and green apples dancing around in the air.

ANOTHER ALPHA?

Trisha

I follow the Alpha Heir—Damon, he said his name was—down a few blocks and over several more, far from where I'd been looking for a hotel. I guess I was really on the wrong track.

We stop at a place that looks really nice—and expensive—and his Beta opens the door for both of us, eyeing me with a smirk for some reason while we head inside.

Damon walks up to the front desk like he owns the place, which I suppose he does being heir to the Alpha King's throne.

"Set up—" He stops and looks at me. "What's your name?"

The lobby is fairly crowded, so I decide to stick with my fake name. I kind of like it anyway. "Daphne," I say. "Daphne Spruce." I have no idea what this Daphne's last name is supposed to be, so I catch sight of the label off a scented candle, and that's the first thing I come up with.

"Set up Ms. Spruce in a good room," Damon says.

"Right away, Alpha Heir Damon," the man behind the counter says, clicking away on his computer screen.

"Put it on my tab."

My mouth falls open, and I turn to Damon to complain, but he and his Beta are out the door before I can get any sound out of my throat. I'd be a little angrier about once again being rescued by a gorgeous man like some helpless damsel in distress if not for the sadness I'm feeling as I notice his scent fade away.

I don't have much time to think about it before the man at the front desk is already handing me a key card. "Room 452, Miss Spruce. The elevators are on your left. Let us know if there's anything you need," he says.

"Thanks." I suppose. I take my bag up to my room, figuring I can probably use a more thorough shower after all that time on the ship where the restrooms weren't very private, so all I could manage was a quick sponge bath here and there.

The hotel shower feels heavenly, and I'm glad for the little bottles of shampoo and conditioner so I don't have to use up any of my own stuff. I really don't know how long I'll be here, or when I'll even think about going home, so I need to use my supplies sparingly. It turns out to be awfully nice shampoo provided by the hotel.

Except that it smells like apples.

I get into some fresh clothes, blow-dry my hair, and sit on what turns out to be a very comfortable couch. But I didn't travel all the way across the ocean to sit in a hotel room. I need to figure out my next step. The two ways I've been 'guided' so far, for lack of better description, are through dreams and a connection with the forest. I've seen enough of this city to know that I'm miles from a forest, and I'm way too wound up to sleep. I'll need to see if I get any dreams later, but right now, I could use a bite to eat.

Downstairs, it's too late for the restaurant, but the bar is open, and from the sound of it, things are getting rowdy. That sounds like fun.

I see him immediately as I walk in. It's hard not to. The whole bar seems to have their undivided attention on the blond sitting at a table right in the middle. He's just as good looking as Damon, in a different way. He's not half as stiff and serious as Damon seemed to be, laughing and joking with a group of guys around him.

A whole group of women stand on the periphery, refilling his drink. They're laughing along with the men's jokes, but the blond seems to be ignoring them.

It seems like he's downing one drink after the other. I wonder why he's not getting plastered at that rate, even though we can handle our alcohol really well as wolves. I can see why as I pass closer and notice there's no alcohol scent at all. But I do smell strawberries everywhere, so it must be fruit juice or something.

It's obvious by the way they're all swooning that he could have any one of these women, or all of them even, but none of them even try to get close because he never looks their way.

I walk past him and up to the bar where I sit on a barstool. I've barely sat down before I smell the strawberries again and feel someone plop into the stool beside me. I turn, and it's the blond. For the first time, I catch sight of his eyes that look like emeralds.

We look at each other for a few more minutes than is comfortable, but for some reason, I can't turn away.

"You don't live here," he finally says.

"What?" I was so lost in his eyes I barely knew he'd spoken.

What's wrong with me?

"Oh, no, I don't," I say.

He laughs. "From the looks of it, you're not from around here at all."

I furrow my brow. "How did you know that?"

He makes a gesture toward my clothes. I look down, realizing for the first time that the styles are a little different here in Green Mountain. It's not a huge difference. In fact, it would take a pretty keen eye to notice. But clearly, those emerald gems are good for a lot more than just mesmerizing people.

"It's okay, though," he says. "If you don't want to advertise it, I won't say anything." He looks at the bartender. "Drinks for the lady, whatever she's having."

"I was just getting something to eat, and I can pay for it," I say. "Thank you, though."

He shrugs. "Just being gentlemanly."

"I like to take care of myself."

He puts his hands up in a mock surrender. "Fair enough."

I order a few snacks that look good enough to get me by as well as a soda. I don't want to drink any alcohol since it might mess with the messages in my dreams. As I'm waiting, he orders some snacks for himself. I guess I made him hungry with the idea of food.

After a few minutes, the bartender gets me a bowl of pretzels and my soda, and the blond guy—I realize I still don't know his name—gets some beer nuts.

I glance back at the table he just left. A few of the women have sat next to the other guys that are there, throwing exaggerated laughs and touching them whenever they get the chance. But a couple of them are staring daggers at me.

I chuckle.

"What's so funny?" he asks.

"I think your girlfriends are a little miffed," I explain.

"They're not my girlfriends," he says roughly. His eyes change a little like he's surprised he just said that.

"Oh, it looked like most of them would rather you not sit with me." I pull my eyes away from the women and look down at my drink.

"That's their problem," he says, taking a bite. "So, what's your name and where are you from?"

I laugh. "You're straightforward, aren't you? I'm... I'm Daphne. And I'm from pretty far from here."

"Pretty far from here, huh? Where is that?" he asks, but it doesn't seem like he's expecting an answer. "I'm Braden."

He reaches out his hand to shake mine, and I take it, trying to be polite in this place where I don't really belong.

But his touch—it's like lightning strikes me. Well, maybe not that intense, but a tingling sensation jolts through me the minute his fingers are around mine. I don't want to let go, and I don't want to look him in the eye because I know I'll burst into a blush. But he's not letting go of my hand, either.

Finally, he does. I stand to leave, almost involuntarily. I have to get out of there, and at the same time, something inside me screams at me to stay. I don't like the feeling. It's like I'm out of control.

"I'd better get going," I say quickly.

"But you haven't eaten your snack," he says.

"I just… I need to leave," I say. "It was nice meeting you, Braden."

I dig through my bag to get some coins, but before I have a chance, he tells the bartender to put it on his tab.

"I can get this," I insist.

"Not while I'm here and can get it for you."

I look at him for a moment and remember I have to get out of there. I'm not even sure why.

I practically run to the elevators, cursing all these good-looking men and their broken doors and bottomless tabs and weird, wonderful scents.

BRADEN

"NOT SURE WHAT that was about, Alpha," the bartender says. "I can have some snacks sent to her room."

I nod, still watching until she turns the corner toward the elevators. She's the most beautiful creature I've ever seen. Her long raven hair is a mess of curls, and all I want to do is run my hands through them while tasting her lips.

I shake my head once her scent, like a field of wildflowers, finally leaves the room.

Now that she's gone, I feel a little differently, like a spell has been broken or something. I've met a lot of beautiful women in my life, but I've never been left so affected by one before.

I look at the bartender. "Do you know where she's from?"

He shrugs. "Alpha King Heir Damon paid for her room. He didn't say anything about her, and I, of course, didn't ask."

Damon—for a split second I feel a twinge of jealousy, but that disappears as fast as I can recognize it. Is she his mate? I don't know how or why, but I'm not really bothered by it if she is, and that's a weird feeling. Something isn't right here, and I need to know what it is.

I gather a handful of beer nuts and stand. "Yes, have a meal sent to her room. It looked like she skipped dinner. On my tab again, of course."

"Yes, Alpha," he says.

I head out the door to find Damon. I know he's here in Oceanside City instead of in his castle in Westmont since Alessandro is back, and I need to ask him about Daphne and figure out what the hell is going on.

8

THE SLUMS OF ROGUE CITY

Rylee

"I WAS JUST THINKING THAT—" I begin.

Calvin cuts me off. "You're not here to think. It's half your sister's fault that the kings sent Ethan and an entire army to kill us all off. Let the men talk."

I'm seething inside, but I let that go. I'm not afraid of Calvin. I could rip his head off in wolf-to-wolf combat if I felt like it, but I know that everyone else fears him. They're willing to do whatever he says just because his father was a fierce warrior. That man is gone now, but everyone is still afraid because Calvin uses trickery to make them think he's as strong as his father.

What a joke.

Since he wants me to let the men talk, I leave them to do just that. It's not them I care about here anyway. I can feel Calvin's eyes staring at me as I walk away. It makes me want to puke, but once again, I try to ignore him.

Outside the circle of warriors, as Calvin calls it, which is really a group of men he has wrapped around his finger, I traipse through the

43

roughshod camp in the damp forest. None of these people belong here. But the problem is that they don't belong anywhere. A good percentage of them don't deserve to be rogues. It wasn't their fault that some family member somewhere along the line messed up and left their pack. Now, their descendants have paid for it dearly.

Most of the 'warriors' have tents, albeit leaky, torn ones. Most are still boys, really, barely eighteen and not even accustomed to their wolves yet. The kings' warriors will rip them to shreds, but Calvin doesn't care.

Past the fighters, things get worse. Families struggle to survive in make-shift lean-tos, or with no shelter at all, just branches or scraps of cloth put together on rickety sticks. Babies cry and their mothers do their best to hush them, knowing Calvin will have the whole family punished if they give away the camp's position.

The situation is bad, but it got this way because of the royals. Alpha King Gene and all those before him expelled people for no reason, or on loose technicalities, and never thought about the consequences to their descendants. The people at the resort keep trying to say that the four new Alpha Kings are so much better because they helped clean up the place, but there are so many others left behind. They must not care either.

Now that the Alpha Kings' son Ethan is here with a massive army, it chills me to think what will happen to all these people.

I ignore the voice inside that sparks to life at the mere thought of Ethan's name. He's just one of the royals, after all.

I reach a lean-to made of woven leaves and vines, and a child runs out. His pants are dirty and in tatters, and he has no shirt.

"Rylee!" His eyes brightening despite his poor condition.

I reach for him and give him a gentle hug. "Hello, Christopher. How are you today?"

He shrugs. "I'm okay. Mom's sick."

My heart sinks, and I quickly look inside the lean-to to see my best friend, Amla, lying on the damp forest floor. I kneel beside her and feel her forehead.

"You're burning up," I say.

"Rylee?" Her voice is weak. "I'll be okay."

"You will not, not here, so you're coming with me to my room at the resort." I've lowered my voice to a whisper. The rogue council here won't let anyone go to the resort or anyplace led by the Alpha Kings, who they are sure are as bad as Gene. The penalty for going there is death. The council tolerates my travels because with my sister in a high position as Isaac's Beta, I can get the information they need.

She shakes her head vigorously. "No, I can't. Father will—"

"Your father will have a healthy daughter who is alive, and he'll thank me for it," I say, interrupting her. "Where's Maya?"

"She went to gather water," Christopher says behind me.

"We'll wait for her," I say firmly. I untie my pouch from my waist and pull out the breadsticks I've brought with me. It's so little, but Christopher's eyes light up when I hand one to him. Amla shakes her head.

"Save that one for Maya," she insists.

"I have enough for all of you. Take it." I know she won't have the strength to walk out of here unless she eats a little something. She hardly looks fit for a walk as it is, but I have to help her.

Maya returns shortly with the water, only a small amount in a rusted old soda can. "Rylee!"

She greets me with a hug. Her thin body looks younger than her ten years. Her brother, just eight, is as small as an average five-year-old. I marvel at how much time has passed. Amla was so young when Maya was born, barely eighteen herself. She's several years older than me, but we've always connected as good friends.

I waste no time getting some food in Maya's belly, though I'm anxious to leave soon. Amla's father is on the council. They usually chat it up and drink their moonshine until after midnight, but there's always the chance they will break it up early, so we have to make a break for it now. I'll carry my friend if I have to just so I can get her and her children the hell out of here.

The least dangerous way out passes somewhat close to the council, but I'm betting on the distraction of the drink to get us by.

Of course, it's not easy to talk Amla into going. We have to argue in the lowest whispers to keep the families nearby from hearing. It could mean bigger rations of food for them if they report 'traitors' to Calvin.

"I can't leave my father," Amla insists. "He'll be alone here."

"He's left you alone here to suffer in sickness," I counter. "If he were any kind of a parent, he would put his needs above your own. You should do the same for your children." I nod toward her kids, who are keeping watch at the edge of the lean-to.

"Are you telling me I don't love my children?" She almost gets too loud with that whisper.

"No, you love them dearly," I say. "And that's why you need to leave with them."

"But that's putting them at risk," she insists.

"Only if we're caught, and we won't get caught." I peek out between the branches. No one has gathered around that I can see. We've done a pretty good job of keeping quiet. "We need to leave soon, though, before the council meeting dies down. Right now, they're too inebriated to care what anyone's doing. Also, the path is downwind of the council meeting area. It's the best possible time."

Reluctantly, she nods. I pull the children into a hug and whisper quietly. "Anything you want to keep, take it now."

They both nod, so terribly wise beyond their years. They've had nothing for so long that I know how much the few trinkets found on the ground might mean to them. Clothes aren't a problem. I'll buy what they need later. But I don't want them to leave any part of their heart behind.

Christopher grabs a tattered old burlap sack filled with his collection of bottle caps he'd always so proudly shown me, and Maya picks up her dirty teddy bear, missing both his eyes and with a good deal of its stuffing falling out.

I know the item Amla wants, so I pick it up myself—her deceased mother's pendant. I make sure she sees me stow it away safely in my sack. She nods, too exhausted to care about anything else she has lying around. I just hope she has the strength to walk.

We split up so it's less obvious, agreeing to meet behind a tree by the path that will take us toward the resort. It was once a narrow road, but now all of the asphalt has crumbled into gravel or dirt, and the forest has overgrown it so it barely functions as a path anymore, but at least it takes us straight in the direction we need to go, and we can slip off it into the forest if we think someone is coming.

We hug again when we meet behind the tree. Amla looks tired and weak, but she also looks determined. I know it's hard for her to leave her father, but now that she's all-in, she'll do anything to keep the kids safe. And so will I.

We reach the part of the path closest to the council meeting. Thankfully, they're all plastered and pretty loud. Their homemade moonshine is strong, and they always drink so much of it that even with a wolf's constant regenerative power, the alcohol wins.

They're loud, and we hear everything they say.

"With this on our side, we can overthrow the Alpha Kings!" Calvin hollers, and the men erupt in cheers.

I don't know what 'this' is, and I normally hate the royals, but I can't help but think that a world with Calvin as Alpha King would be ten times worse.

Ethan

"The scouts have found their camp," my cousin reports.

"Good," I say. "We'll have the warriors take it, then."

Isaac shakes his head. "We can't. These losers drag their families with them everywhere they go. There are a few fighters and a whole slum filled with women, children, and the elderly."

I pause, surprised, but then suggest, "Well, surely, they'd want help. We could just go in and offer them shelter and food."

"We've tried that before." I turned at the sound of Katherine's voice. "Their trick is to make sure we can't attack because the innocent will always be in the way."

I fold my arms. "That sounds pathetic, yet organized. Who's running all that?"

"Intel says his name is Calvin," Katherine continued. "We have no idea what his last name is or where he came from, but he seems to have a strong hold on these people."

"Well, we're not going to attack innocents, that's for sure." I sigh. "And now we have a new mission. If there are families out there living in slums, we need to help them."

"I have tried," Isaac says. "Any connection to the Alpha Kings makes them shut down. They won't listen to a thing we say."

"There's got to be a way," I insist. "We need to find someone who can speak to them on their own level, someone connected to them." I look around at Isaac, Katherine, and the lead warriors gathered around us. "Any suggestions?"

9

THE NORTHERN SECTOR

Braden

I HEAD OUTSIDE. The air is crisp, and the sky above is clear, the kind of night I love. But my head really is a mess, though it did seem to clear a bit once Daphne's scent faded. I'm not usually one to react to a woman like that. I like to have fun, of course, but I never go ga-ga over someone.

What the hell is a ga-ga?

I must still be in a bit of a fog.

"Braden?" Andrew asks from behind me.

"Damn, I forgot you were in there." I rub my temples.

"You forgot your Beta." It's a statement, not a question. "Are you feeling okay? It's not like you were even drinking."

I look at him, and he seems to read something in my eyes, which he's annoyingly very good at doing.

"That woman." It's another statement. "What was she, your mate or something?"

I shake my head. "No, she couldn't be. I mean, I caught her scent, felt her pull, but there was something stopping that, like it was only half there."

"Well, I didn't get a good look at her, but she may not have her wolf yet," he says. "That would make it half a bond, wouldn't it?"

I shrug. "The hell if I know. She seemed to feel something too, though. If she didn't have her wolf, how would she feel anything?"

"I have no clue." He looks at me like I've lost my mind. "Maybe she's the Princess of Sheba or something."

"Where the hell is Sheba?"

"Wherever your head's at right now." He laughs. "Look, we'd better go find her."

"Who?"

"Your mate, Alpha Braden," he says. "Honestly, do I have to do all the thinking for you?"

"Daphne can't be my mate." I frown. Just saying the sentence feels so wrong.

"Oh, for the love of the Goddess, of course, she is," he says. "I've seen you with women from the east shore to the northern tundra, and you've never once rubbed your temple over one."

"What? There are no women up north."

"I was just—" He stops. "Never mind. Braden, what were you doing outside?"

"Oh, I need to go talk to Damon and Alessandro," I explained. "They're at the pub on North Second Street."

"Alessandro's back?"

I nod. "Just got in this morning, I think. You'd better come along, unless that blonde in the hotel bar has you enthralled."

"Not enough to leave my confused Alpha wandering Oceanside City." He opens the door of my SUV, which my driver just brought around. I don't remember mind-linking him, so Andrew must have taken care of that himself.

It's only a few blocks to Damon's favorite pub. I try to get my head in the game and forget about Daphne for now. Alessandro just got back from Dark Forest and probably has some intel we can use to keep Damon's father from making an ass out of all of us by attacking the place. As an Alpha, I need to put my people above every other distraction, no matter how beautiful she looks, or if she smells like wildflowers.

My tactic doesn't work well, though, because the moment I walk in and see Damon, I'm greeted with a phrase that almost knocks me to the floor.

"I think that Daphne might be my mate."

TRISHA

THE WHOLE WORLD IS ROCKING, and I realize I'm on a ship, but it looks different than the one I took to Green Mountain. I get up from my bed and open a door, and suddenly, I'm in a room with a bunch of men playing cards. I try to look at them closer, but they have no faces. One has dark, straight hair and the other two are blond. I open my mouth to speak to them, but they're gone just as quickly as they showed up.

I turn around, and I'm in a forest. There's a little boy calling. He needs help. I start running, but the more I run, the further away he sounds. But then, he's right in front of me, in a village, and there's snow everywhere.

"Help us," he says.

I inhale sharply as I sit up in bed, my heart pounding. The dreams are getting downright strange. I grab my notebook and try to write down everything I remember before I forget. I remember being on a ship, and watching a poker game, but I can't remember who was playing at all anymore. I remember a little boy out in the cold in a village.

He must be who I'm meant to save. I need to find a way to get to him.

I stare up at my ceiling for a while, stewing about how Damon put my room on his tab, and then how Braden swooped in and started paying for food for me. I couldn't believe it when the hotel staff brought a full meal for me to my room last night and wouldn't let me pay for it. I didn't blame them since they had Alpha's orders, but it annoyed me. If I wanted to be waited on hand and foot and not have to pay for anything, I could have stayed back at the castle in Dark Forest.

I get up and take another shower, not sure how long I'll be traveling if I'm going to ever find the little boy and his snowy village, so I figure I might as well enjoy the comforts of home while I've got a chance. Then I notice that while the hotel shampoo smells like apples, the conditioner smells like strawberries.

Great.

I get dressed and make my way downstairs to the hotel diner. This time, I pay for my own meal of pancakes, eggs, and toast. It's more than I usually eat, but again, I'm not sure what's ahead for me. The buttermilk pancakes are good enough that the Goddess herself could eat them.

I turn in my keycard and thank the guy at the desk, heading out into the city streets. This is a nice town, or at least, this seems to be a nice part of town. I'm not going to get anywhere here, but I don't want to get lost, so I figure my first stop is buying a map.

Looking around, I'm really not sure where they sell them, so I head back into the hotel and inquire at the desk.

"What sector do you want, miss?" the man says.

"Sector?"

"Yes." I can see he's trying hard to be patient with me, but since this is a port city, he must be used to strangers asking silly questions. "The west sector has Greenhaven and several of the college towns. The south sector has Seaview and most of the resort locations. We're in the east sector, with the port city here, and of course, the open ocean in front."

"Which sector has snow?" I ask.

He furrows his brow. "Snow?"

"Yes, which one is cold, where it snows?"

"Miss, I'm afraid it only snows in the north sector, but there's nothing there to map out, so I don't have one of those," he says.

I frown. "No villages or towns at all?"

He shrugs. "I suppose that's possible, but I've never heard of one. No one ever goes there."

"How would I get there to see for myself?" I ask.

"Oh, miss, you don't want to go there," he insists. "It's very dangerous. I hear there are criminals there because no one dares travel that way, except of course, for the unsavory characters from Northside."

"What's Northside?" I ask.

He looks a little shaky and adjusts his tie. "Oh, that's nothing," he says. "Don't worry about that place. You should stay as far away from there as possible, miss."

I get the feeling he's done telling me anything, so I buy the three maps he's offered and head outside again, hailing a cab. If there's anyone who can tell me about this place, it's going to be a cab driver.

The yellow taxi pulls up, and I step inside.

"Where to, miss?" the man asks. He looks older than my parents, so he probably knows the place well.

"I need to get to Northside," I explain.

He has sort of the same response as the hotel clerk, as if he's instantly nervous. "Why would a single, young gal like you want to go there?"

I know for sure I need to get there now. It's the only way I know of to get to this mysterious north sector, which has to be where the little boy and his village are located. I worry that the cab driver won't take me if I have no reason to go there, so I make up something.

"My father is there," I lie. "I'm supposed to meet him."

"Oh, well, that's different," he says. "But my route doesn't go that far out of Oceanside City. There's a bus station on the north side of the port, though. I can take you there if you'd like."

"Yes, please," I say. I've never ridden on a bus before. Some of my friends did growing up, but I always had an escorted ride to school. "Do you know how much a ticket there will cost?"

"Can't say for sure, miss," he says. "But the fares are pretty reasonable."

I nod as he drives through the city. I recognize some of the streets as ones where I first started to explore and go shopping. Apparently, the bus depot is close to the shopping district.

When he drops me off, I give him the fare and a good tip and head inside. The terminal is crowded, and it reminds me of the stories my parents will never let me forget—how they stopped and searched all the trains for me and my siblings, only to have me be the one baby they couldn't find for a long time.

I know that was a horrible time for Mom. I can see it in her face whenever she tells me the story, which is often. I feel a twinge of guilt because I'm currently missing again, and I don't have a way to tell her I'm okay. I have a feeling that if I write a letter, they'll send the whole kingdom's army after me.

I stand in line for a while before I get to the window where I grab a postcard, just in case I feel like sending it. "One-way ticket to Northside, please."

THE SEER OF RAVEN PACK

Rylee

IT'S nighttime before we get back to the resort, and I send the guard on a quick errand so I can get Amla and the kids inside. After I deal with him, I meet up with my friends again in the hallway and sneak them all up to my room.

Christopher and Maya look around with wide eyes. I can't even imagine how they feel. They've always been on the run living as rogues, but when their father was alive, he provided for them fairly well. They were probably too young at the time to remember that. Now, all they know is hardship, so this simple room must be a shock.

Calvin and their father Ajax were best friends, and they left their pack together. There was some sort of argument with the Alpha. Of course, he dragged Amla and the babies along. They started gathering rogues from all over, and at first, their skirmishes with packs were all about their egos. But then Ajax died in one of those battles, and instead of blaming himself, Calvin forced all the men and boys in the group to train to fight, even taking on the Alpha Kings' territories.

Amla was too distraught from the loss of her mate to do anything but follow him.

I've tried to ask them all many times to stop fighting and just help everyone live well, but Calvin doesn't care, so I've been trying to do it all myself ever since. Calvin let his best friend's family rot, and it disgusts me.

I guess there aren't many good men left in the world.

I look at my friend and her children and don't know where to start. They need to be cleaned up, fed, and clothed, and Amla needs medical attention. I can't risk taking her to the healer because they'd ask too many questions. I decide that food is the most critical thing right now, as well as rest for Amla.

"I need you to stay here and be very quiet," I say. "No one comes in my quarters, so just keep the door locked, and you won't be bothered. Stay away from the windows and keep the curtains closed. I'll use my key when I come in. I need to go get you something to eat. I promise I'll be right back."

All three of them nod, and I go out the door, locking it behind me. The first order of business is food. I need to give them something nourishing, maybe some soup. Though there are a few other people in the kitchen, I don't worry since people often take food to their families throughout the resort. I get out a tray and load it up with some bowls of soup and fresh bread, and I grab some milk for the kids and the kind of tea bag I always use when I'm feeling under the weather, along with a cup of hot water.

No one asks me about any of it, and no one is in the hallways right now, so I get the tray back to the room with no problem. I feel bad when the kids are eating because they're so hungry they try to eat the hot soup too fast.

"Start with the bread," I suggest, though I know they can't eat too much of anything too fast until they're used to it.

I set Amla up in my bed propped with pillows and give her some soup and the tea.

It's not long before the bowls and cups are empty. They're all so hungry and exhausted that I decide the cleanup can wait until everyone has had a little rest.

"Rylee, what are we going to do?" Amla asks as I tuck the blankets around her.

I shake my head. "We'll worry about that later. Lean back. Get some rest. We'll talk when you're feeling better. You're all safe here."

She nods, so exhausted that she can't argue with anything right now. She lays her head back, and I grab some pillows and blankets from the closet for the kids. Even sleeping on blankets on the floor is a huge improvement from the cold, damp forest.

I sit in the chair for a bit watching them all drift off to sleep. I know I can never go back to the rogue encampment now. I've burned that bridge, blown it up even. Images of some of the other people I'd been trying to help flicker through my mind, and it stings to know I'll probably never see them again. Calvin will be furious and will no doubt launch an unwinnable attack immediately, hoping to get to me.

I've always thought my sister was a fool for taking up with the royals and getting her high-ranked position. I used to tell her to be careful with who she trusted, and she always insisted that Alpha Isaac had our best interests at heart.

I suppose now I'm going to have to trust her and pray to the Goddess that the Alphas aren't as bad as I've been told.

ETHAN

ALPHA ISAAC HAD some snacks brought out to the fire pit after dinner. We've all gathered around it on benches, with several top-ranking warriors and their families relaxing in the warmth. It's nice to talk with my aunt again, and with my cousins. It's been a long time since we've seen each other.

I just wish we were here just for the company. It's troubling when rogues attack. My dads hate to have to fight them because they know they're not trained nearly as well as our warriors, so it's not a fair fight, but we can't just allow them to attack villages and hurt others.

I'm working with Jeremiah, who will be my Beta once Matthew and I take over from our dads, to develop a program for the families of rogues. I know it's sort of a Luna duty, but they don't have a pack, so their affairs don't really fall under any of the Lunas, though Mom does everything she can to help whenever someone comes forward.

The main problem is that they all stay in hiding, so it's been hard for her to help a good number of them. I know the rogues are worried about what we'll do to them when they get caught, but my dads and all of us know that, for most of them, it's not their fault they don't have a pack. Gene was a horrible ruler, and though his father is now a kind old man, he was old-fashioned about who could stay in a pack or not back when he was in charge. That means that one wolf may have been kicked out of his pack years ago, but his family is still paying for it by being stuck without a real home.

I hope that when I find my mate, she'll be the kind of Luna who will help everyone in the kingdom, including the rogues, just like my mother.

For some reason, my thoughts turn to the raven-haired beauty with the silver flakes in her eyes.

But Isaac interrupts my thoughts. "You look a thousand miles away, cousin."

I chuckle, snapping out of it to look at him. His mate, Chelene, has red hair brighter than ours, which I'd never thought possible. They look so happy together, holding hands and sitting close on the bench while they each hold separate conversations. Chelene is chatting with my Aunt Kelly, and Kelly's mate, Corbin, is talking to one of the warriors while still holding her hand. I know it's going to be wonderful to have a mate like that one day.

Isabelle stands. "Well, it's getting a little late for us pregnant folks." She giggles. "It was good to see all of you. Ethan, I hope you're around for a while. I don't get to see my cousin much."

I stand as well and give her a one-armed hug. "I'll see you in the morning. I'll be here for a while, maybe long enough to see my… what do they call a cousin's baby?"

"First cousin maybe?" Kelly says. "Something like that."

"Well, hopefully I get to see… him or her?"

"Him." Isabelle's mate, Stan, smiles wide.

"Hopefully, I'll get to see him while I'm here," I continue. "It looks like it won't be long now."

"A couple of weeks tops, I pray to the Goddess," she says with another giggle. "Goodnight, everyone."

"Goodnight."

When she and Stan walk away, everyone goes back to their conversations. I'm quiet for now, just enjoying seeing everyone in my family so happy with their mates, until a woman sits next to me. I turn to look at her. Her hair, fading red with a few white streaks, shimmers in the flickering fire light. Her eyes are green with amber circles around them and seem deep with wisdom.

"Young Alpha," she says. "I'm happy you're with us tonight."

"Thank you." I hold out my hand. "I'm sorry. I don't know your name."

"Because we haven't been introduced," she says. She takes my hand and shakes it firmly. "I'm Aerona, seer of the Raven pack."

It's only been a year since we decided to separate the resort pack from Beach, my father's pack. It made sense since it was so far away and needed a separate government. Isaac had just met his mate, so it was the perfect time for him to run things. They found the name Raven on some of the old resort equipment, though that wasn't the name of the resort itself.

"I didn't know my cousin's pack had a seer. Were you in the original group who joined Beach pack?"

She shakes her head. "No, I found my way here many years ago when your aunt and uncle were running things here. I'd never seen it as it was when it was rundown, but I do have visions."

"Visions of the past? Don't you see the future?"

"No, my gift is a bit different," she explains. "I believe my place is to see the past so that it's not repeated in the future, if it involves evil, that is."

"Interesting," I say. "I've never met anyone like you."

She giggles. "You have, you just don't remember. You were just a little baby when I first saw you. You see, I was one of the girls brought to Dark Forest castle for the competition. I was on the train with Rose, and we spoke… well, as much as we could at the time. About a year after you were born, I went to visit her. She suggested I come here to help out once she learned of my gift."

"I had no idea," I say.

"I was so nervous that day on the train," she continues. "We all were. I didn't have my seer skills yet, not until I got my wolf later that year. I wish I'd had them at the time so I could see King Gene's true self before your mother had to suffer so, especially with the kidnappings of your four as newborns. She's such a nice lady and a wonderful Luna Queen."

I nod. "She is."

It suddenly felt like my wolf jolted awake, and I turn to see Katherine's sister walk over to her and whisper in her ear.

MATE OF THREE ALPHAS?

Damon

"We'd better not be talking about the same Daphne."

I turn to see Braden walking in with his Beta. He pulls up a chair from the table next to ours, and Andrew heads to the bar to order drinks.

"What?" I ask.

"If you're talking about the Daphne you put up in the hotel, it's impossible," he explains. "She's my mate."

Alessandro and I both start laughing. The look on his face is price-less, and the bigger his eyes get in confusion, the more I can't hold back the laugh.

"I don't know what's so funny, but you two have thirty seconds before I rip your eyes out," he says.

I hold up my hand. "Hey, man, it's okay. Relax. I'll explain as soon as I—" That's it. Just the idea of explaining it to him has me in stitches, and normally I'm a pretty serious guy. I have to be with the whole kingdom relying on me.

But this is damn funny, and I just start laughing again. I can't help it. I know I need to let him in on it right away, but whenever Braden is both confused and mad, he makes the most contorted faces that crack me up. It's been that way since we were all kids.

Braden stands, pushing the chair out with his thigh muscles and balling his fist like he's going to hammer me. That helps push me out of my laughing fit, and I hold up both hands this time.

"Look, Alessandro and I have been here for quite a while talking about this," I say. "So, we've had more time to get used to it."

"Get used to what?"

"That Daphne is all our mates," I explain.

"What?!"

He still looks like he wants to punch me.

"Well, at first I thought it was me and Alessandro, but obviously there's something going on with you too," I add.

"That's not possible." It's a statement, and he says it while sitting back down in his chair.

I had the same reaction earlier. I'd been about ready to tear Alessandro to shreds for even thinking about touching my mate, but that feeling disappeared in just seconds. I was left wondering what was happening, until Alessandro said he'd felt the same way. We've decided that she is both of our mates for whatever reason, and the Moon Goddess must know what she's doing.

"They have the same thing in Dark Forest," Alessandro explains. "All four Alphas are mates with the Luna queen."

"Well, that's ridiculous. And that's Dark Forest for you. Something like that would never happen here." He leans back and folds his arms, though I can tell he's coming to the same conclusion as Alessandro and me. "Besides, Daphne isn't royal."

Alessandro shakes his head. "That's right, she's Roland's daughter. He's a merchant. But then, the Luna Queen in the other kingdom wasn't a royal either at first, just mated to four Alphas."

"I don't think Daphne has her wolf yet, either," I say. "So that's probably why the pull is so faint, yet it's clearly there. She doesn't feel it yet."

"I didn't sense her wolf either," Alessandro says. "Yet she's very strong and capable. It's almost as though she's been professionally trained."

"But that's for royalty, too," Braden argues. "None of this makes sense."

"I agree." I take a sip of my drink. "But there's one thing all three of us know. There's something about her, and we all feel it. I don't think we'll know for sure until she gets her wolf. Until then, we need to keep her safe. When I ran into her last, she was in trouble with some guys cornering her in an alley. That's why I made sure she got to the hotel."

"Is she still there now?" Alessandro asks.

"She is that I know of," Braden says.

I look up to see the man who was behind the desk at the hotel walk in, and I wave him over.

"Alpha, it's a pleasure to see you," he says.

"Thank you," I nod. "Same to you. Say, I was wondering if you know how many days the woman I checked in is planning on staying."

"The one with the curly dark hair?" he asks.

"Yes, that's the one," I confirm.

"Oh, my, what a looker," he says. He closes his eyes as if savoring her in his mind, and I can feel my wolf growl dangerously. And then he continues. "Those beautiful eyes were like the Goddess herself had created her from gold and diamonds. I'd never seen hair that deep black and that curly. It certainly made those eyes pop. I wanted to run my fingers through it. And that lovely body. I—"

He opens his eyes then to see three very angry Alphas just about ready to jump up, shift, and rip his throat off.

"Um... oh, yeah, um... I... well—" He clears his throat. "Sorry, but she actually checked out already."

All three of us stand, the sound of our chairs scraping across the floor drawing every eye to our table.

"Checked out?!" Braden is the closest, so he is in the guy's face.

He gulps loudly. "I... I didn't know I was supposed to.... She just left, I mean, how was I to stop her?"

I take a breath, trying to calm the rage that radiates through my veins. "Do you know where she was headed?"

"Well I... I did inquire with the cab driver after he got back," the man says. "I was just curious, that's all. I mean, she's a lovely woman and—" Alessandro cracks his knuckles, and the man's eyes go wide. "She went to the bus station to get a ticket to Northside."

At that, all three of us grab our jackets and run out the door. I don't know how, but I manage to have the clarity of mind to throw several dollars down on the table first to pay the bill.

But after that, the only clarity I have is getting to Daphne however we need to do it.

Our mate is in Northside, and we need to get to her.

Now.

⸻

TRISHA

I GUESS I should have thought things through a little more before I got on the bus. Stepping off, I'm immediately met with a cold, biting wind, and there's snow on the ground, though I'm luckily wearing some pretty sturdy shoes. A heavier coat and some boots would have been nice, though.

I turn around to thank the bus driver, and the door is already shut and he's pulling away. He makes a wide turn in the roundabout and heads back the way we came, a bit faster than when we pulled in, I notice.

Great.

Well, maybe I can find a store that's open and buy some better clothes here. I turn around and look at the small bus depot for a moment, which is little more than a shack, and decide I'm better off walking down the road. Maybe there's a store nearby.

But just a few steps later I realize what I've gotten myself into. There aren't any stores. There aren't any buildings even. And there certainly aren't any people, just a barren landscape with blowing snow.

After realizing this, I head back toward the bus depot and go inside. The door creaks heavily but thankfully opens. Inside, it's empty, and only a single lightbulb flickers in the corner. There's a booth to buy tickets, or at least there seems to be a place where people used to buy tickets because now, it's full of cobwebs.

"Hello?" My voice echoes, and I'm instantly regretting that I said anything. There are a couple of doors to restrooms, and Goddess knows who's in there. I don't hear anything or catch any scents, but this whole place gives me the creeps.

Knowing what's outside, I figure it's best to hang out here for a bit. I don't have my wolf, and who knows how many miles I'll have to walk to get to some sort of city, or at least a small village, or maybe just a single house that's heated and doesn't have murderers living in it.

Yes, that would be good.

I guess I'll look around. I go ahead and try the restrooms, and they're just small one-stall spaces that nobody is in, or has been in for some time, I guess, given how filthy they are, so at least those murderers I'm worried about aren't here.

I notice a desk at the other end of the room which I suppose is where people used to check in after buying their tickets. There's a section to lift up and get behind it, so I do that, hoping someone left some unopened snacks since there doesn't seem to be any vending machines or anything here, not that I'd expect them to have anything in them.

What I do find is a box marked Lost and Found. It's a pretty big box and a little dusty, but I figure no one's been here in a long time so whatever is in it is long lost.

Amazingly, I find a coat—a warm one. It's one of those puffer jackets, way too big for me but definitely the kind of thing that'll keep me warm for a long walk to wherever I'm going. I also can't believe I'm lucky enough to find some boots, and these are actually only half a size too big, so they'll do. I check to be sure they're not dirty inside and slip them on, throwing my own shoes in the box, just to give something back.

Wrapped in my warm coat and comfortable with my boots and extra socks I found, I decide it's time to brave the cold and find somewhere to go in this place. I trudge out the door and look around. I could go either way, so I decide to go right, which is in the direction away from the street the bus brought me on, which must lead into town, or something.

There's really nothing out here but fields of snow and a road that's somehow staying relatively free of the powdery stuff because the wind keeps blowing it away. It's cold, but the coat is really doing its job, and I figure I can walk like this for several miles before I start to get tired. Hopefully, I find something by then so I can rest and get something to eat. If not, I suppose I'll have to turn around and go back to the bus depot.

I'm a few miles down the road when I hear a car coming up behind me. A slight shiver goes down my spine. This is either good news or bad, and I pray to the Goddess that it's the former.

The car slows to a stop just behind me.

1 2

———

THE WAR CRY

Alpha King Rohan

"We attack at dawn!" I bellow.

I hold my hand up in the air dramatically, making a fist. My head is aloft, eyes focused on the sky to ensure that the Moon Goddess herself has heard my war cry.

And no one says anything.

I lower my hand and look around, and I'm alone in the room. What the fuck?

"Kurt!" This time it's more of a scream than a bellow.

He's out of breath by the time he gets here. How the fuck far away was he?

"What is it, Your Majesty?" he says between pants.

I put my hand on my hip. "I've just declared war, you idiot! My presentation was impeccable, and now I have to do it again! What kind of a Beta misses it when his Alpha King declares war because he's off twiddling his thumbs?"

He takes a few more breaths as if he's trying to find an answer for that. Instead, he says, "Rowan—"

"You'll address me as Your Majesty!" I cut him off.

I catch him rolling his eyes. He does that a lot, since we were kids.

But he can't go around acting like he can still call me by my first name just because he remembers that I liked Skylar in the third grade. She was pretty, with bright red hair and green eyes that sparkled when she looked at me. Her voice was like—"

"Your Majesty…?"

Oh, he kicked me out of a good memory this time. She'd kissed me on the cheek behind the bleachers. Oh, what a kiss….

"We don't have word from the spies yet," he says, insisting on interrupting my thoughts again. "I thought Your Majesty would wait until they returned."

"I don't need spies to tell me what I already know!" I scream. I think better of that quickly since all the bellowing has already hurt my throat. I lower my voice. He's right in front of me, after all. "Dark Forest is evil. Just look at the name! What kind of a place is named that!" I clear my throat, assume my position with my fist in the air, and repeat, "We attack at dawn!"

He bites his bottom lip and just stands there for a second. "Ro— Your Majesty, it'll take weeks to get the fleet there, and that's after we've assembled all the troops and weapons."

I frown. "Well, dawn on the day we arrive, of course."

"But what if we get there later in the afternoon?" he asks.

I want to slap him. I just might. "You will order the ships to arrive at dawn! I don't care what it takes! That low-life scum of a kingdom is going to be destroyed, and I'll be the one to do it! At dawn, we attack as ordered!"

He stands there with his mouth open for a few minutes before mumbling, "Yes, Your Majesty," and then he walks away.

I go over to my mini-bar and pull out my special tea. The seer Coraline has been giving me this special tea for about ten years now. It's made with a bunch of different leaves—she hasn't told me which ones—and it doesn't taste very good, but she promised it would help me see things clearer. Sometimes, I think it makes my mind wander. But other times, I think it makes me smarter. I'm convinced that I really do see the kingdom of Green Mountain now for what it really is—a true enemy.

I've asked Coraline about that, and she always says that my vision is clear now, so that must be true.

I hold my fist to the air again, this time in a silent war cry. I'll show Dark Forest that the kingdom of Green Mountain is nothing to mess with! It's their own fault for being the dirty thieves and con artists that Coraline says they are.

Their evil ways end here! Well, over there, I suppose. But either way, they will end!

Rylee

Amla seems to be getting worse since I ran out of the remedy that I got last month from the healer, Maddie. I don't want to let her in on my secret about Amla and the kids, so somehow, I'll need to get her to tell me what it's made of and where she gets it.

I call Christopher and Maya over to the corner of the room. For now, Amla is asleep.

"I need you to keep an eye on your mother," I tell them. "I have to go get her some more medicine. You need to be as quiet as you can, and please don't look out the windows. Can you do that for me?"

They both nod, and with everything they've gone through, I know I can trust them. I lock the door behind me and head to Maddie's office. I find her there, her black hair up in a bun as she stares at some papers on her desk.

"Rylee," she says, "it's good to see you."

"You as well," I say, sitting in the chair in front of her. "I was wondering if I could get more of your fever remedy."

Her expression doesn't change. "You don't look ill."

"It's for a friend."

She nods, knowingly. "I see. I've known you for a long time, and I trust you, so I won't ask questions. If you're looking for more of it, then someone must truly need it."

I nod back, not wanting to say more.

"Unfortunately, I'm out until the next shipment," she says. "But if you need it badly, you can use the raw ingredient for it, which is the bark of the cherish tree."

I shake my head. "I'm not familiar with that."

She holds up a finger and spins around, pulling a book off the shelf, then walks around to my side of the desk and flips pages. "Right here." She points to a picture. "There's a grove of those just east of the compound."

"I've seen those." I stand to leave. "How do I administer it?"

"Just have the patient chew on a small piece of the bark for about ten minutes, then spit it out." She holds her fingers up to show the size of the piece. "Follow up with water. Do that about four times per day."

"Thank you," I say, leaving.

"Rylee?"

I turn around.

"Be careful."

I nod and walk out the door, heading east. I find the trees quickly and begin to scrape off pieces of the bark and put them in my pocket.

"Are you okay?"

I whirl around at the sound of the voice. I'm startled, but I have a strange feeling inside, like I want to hear that voice again. But then I see it's just the royal who came out to 'save' us all, Ethan. I must be feeling confused because he's very attractive, but then, most of the royals are. I have to remember that I can't trust them.

"I'm fine. Why?" I ask.

He points to the tree. "My mother always gave me cherish tree compound when I had a fever. But you don't look feverish."

"It's for a friend." I turn around and keep scraping.

Why would a royal get cherish tree bark? They have more expensive treatments they can use. Just when I think he might be walking away, he appears in front of me and gets out a pocket knife to start scraping—on the same tree!

My nose catches a whiff of his scent. It's definitely birchwood, my favorite. It's probably some expensive aftershave he bought with all his royal money.

"I've got this," I say.

"I'm just trying to help," he replies and keeps on scraping.

Damn, he smells good. My wolf stirs inside, but I don't sense a wolf in him. He must not have found his wolf yet. So why is he so damn distracting? I scrape faster so I can get out of here.

"Ow!"

I jump back and drop my knife, holding onto my now-bleeding arm. I can't believe I cut myself, allowing myself to get so distracted by a royal.

But before I can do anything else, he's right in front of me, ripping his shirt and tying a piece around my arm. I'm getting blood all over him, and Goddess, his bare chest ripples with muscles. I want to run my fingers over them.

What's wrong with me?

"I-I'm fine." I look at my arm, and he's done a more than competent job of tying it up. "Thank you. You seem to know your stuff."

He nods. "My fathers taught us all field medicine for combat."

"Us?"

"Me and my brother and two sisters," he explains.

Oh, yes, the royal quads. I forgot there were so many of them.

"Here, you'd better sit for a minute. You lost a lot of blood there." He leads me to a fallen tree and sits me on it. "It takes longer to heal when that happens."

I nod, knowing that. "How do you know about the bark? You're a royal."

He chuckles. "You say that like it's a disease."

I shrug.

He laughs then turns serious. "Well, my mother is different."

"She's an Alpha's daughter, isn't she?" I know only Alphas' daughters were considered royal breeders back in the day. I'm glad they don't do that anymore.

"She is, but she was poorly mistreated, up until she came to the

Dark Forest castle. She used to have to find her own medicine whenever she got sick when she was little."

"That's terrible," I say.

He shrugs. "It is. I never knew her when her life was like that, but she never forgot. She always tries to be sure all the people in the kingdom have better lives. She doesn't want anyone to go through what she did."

"But that's not—"

"Not what?" he asks.

"Nothing." I've always been told Luna Queen Rose didn't do anything but buy new clothes for herself.

"Anyway, she taught me about all the plants she used so that if I ever ran into anyone who needed help I could at least help them find the right medicine for whatever was wrong," he continues.

I look up at him. His eyes are so beautiful, bright green to go with his red hair. I even notice different shades of red in each of the strands now that I'm up close. "Even rogues?"

He nods. "That's exactly who she meant. It always bothered her that there were so many people out there who had been kicked out of their packs. She wondered what happened to their spouses and children. It worried her a lot that she couldn't help them because they were so afraid of the way things used to be that they didn't reach out for help. It wasn't their fault they were out there surviving on their own. Hell, it wasn't even their family members' fault they were kicked out half the time. The world under Alpha King Gene was a terrible place, apparently."

Is this true, I wonder? Is the Luna Queen really a kind person who'd been mistreated herself and now wanted the best for everyone, including rogues?

I'm starting to wonder whether the royals are as bad as I've been told.

13

THREE MATES?

Trisha

WITH ALL THE BLOWING SNOW, I've been sticking to the road to be sure I'm going straight and not wandering in circles. But I rethink that idea when the car stops behind me.

I'm torn between running away and facing whoever it is. I don't have a single weapon on me, but I've been training to fight almost as long as I've been walking, and holding my own in a house with two brothers has only made me tougher.

But it's a calculated risk. If whoever is following me can shift, or if there are more than a few people in that car, then I'm history.

I figure, "What the hell?" and turn around.

The engine shuts off, and I swallow nervously. The car windows are too darkly tinted to see inside. When the doors open, I catch such a strong whiff of strawberries and apples that I start to get a little dizzy.

Oh, no.

It's not.

It can't be.

But it is—out steps Damon, with a look on his face like he just found his lost puppy. He runs up to me, and I notice the other car doors open but don't even look to see who it is.

"Are you kidding me?" I ask, exasperated. "What are you doing here?"

"Well, that's a fine way to greet your rescuers," he says.

"Rescue? Do I look like I need to be rescued?"

"Well, actually… um, yes." He chuckles, and if his eyes weren't as blue as the ocean, I'd punch him.

"Sorry to disappoint, but the damsel here is perfectly un-distressed," I say, whirling around to walk away.

"Is that a word?" he asks.

I raise up my hand to wave at him, not looking back. "It is now!"

"But Daphne…."

I freeze in place, my waving hand still stuck in the air at the sound of the new voice. It's sexy, deep and gravelly, and the last time I heard it, I was on a ship.

I take a breath and turn around to see Alessandro's mesmerizing silver eyes.

"What the—what are you doing here?" I ask.

"Getting you out of here," he says.

"Why? I'm perfectly fine," I insist. "You two know each other, I'm guessing. Was there a sale on strawberry and apple cologne?"

They look at each other.

"What do you mean?" Alessandro asks.

"Never mind." I turn around again and start walking, but I hear—and feel—their footsteps behind me.

What is with these guys?

"Daphne, it's dangerous up here in Northside."

It's a third voice, and another one I recognize. I don't even need to turn around. "Braden. You're here too. What are you guys, a posse of sexy hunks straight out of Alpha's Quarterly?" I instantly regret saying that, and I'm not even sure why I did, so I just keep walking forward.

Maybe they'll leave.

But I don't want them to.

My cheeks are burning red, and I can't possibly turn around and look at Braden, though I wouldn't mind a peek at those gorgeous muscles.

What am I saying?

"She thinks we're sexy," Alessandro says.

I can feel him smirking even though I can't see him. I want to slap him. But I also want to run over to him and jump up into his arms.

Yep, there's something seriously wrong with me.

I put my hands on my cheeks, hoping that my near-frostbite will fight back the blush, but I'm so annoyed right now that I don't even care. "Are you really that full of yourself?"

"He is." There's not a hint of a smile on Braden's face when I steal a glance, and that almost makes me laugh until I remember I'm supposed to be mad at these guys for following me.

"Hey!" Alessandro protests.

Braden shrugs. "Well, it's true."

"As if you're not the one with a shit-eating grin on your face, surrounded by bimbos half the time," Alessandro argues.

"What? I can't help it if they hang around me," Braden says. "It's not like I pay any attention to them, and I certainly won't now that I found my mate."

The phrase panics me for some reason. If he's found his mate, why is he out here bothering me? Yet, the idea that he has a mate has me screaming inside.

Why would I care about that?

I'm seriously going to need to talk to the castle counselor when I get back home.

They keep arguing, and Damon walks over to them to try to deal with that while I start slowly backing up. I'm about twenty yards away when I figure they're too busy arguing with each other to notice me, so I spin around and take off running.

In my head, I want to get away, but my heart and my body are begging me to stop. It's the strangest sensation, and I'm not sure what to think of it. I've never felt this way before.

Still, I keep running. I don't know any of these guys well enough to trust them, though something tells me I should.

I'm already getting tired of all these strange feelings. I'm starting to think that something about Green Mountain messes with your head. Maybe that's why we've always been told to stay away from here.

I'm putting some good distance between me and the guys when I feel my foot twist. Everything else happens in slow motion. I look down and see my foot caught in a pothole, then I start falling forward. I feel myself going airborne since I'd been running so fast, and quick as a flash, silver fur blocks my fall, and I dive into the wolf, grabbing hold of him to keep from stumbling over.

My face lands smack in the middle of his fur, and the scent of apples and strawberries floats into my nose.

"Are you all right?"

I look up to see Damon standing over me, reaching a hand down to help me up.

It takes me a moment, but I snap out of the surprise, looking down at the silver fur and realizing that it's Alessandro's wolf.

"Oh, for Goddess's sake," I say, pushing off the wolf and standing, brushing myself off. "Why are you guys so persistent?"

"Why are you running away from us?"

The gravelly voice comes from behind me, and I spin around ready to yell at Alessandro, but all I see is a stunning, tall and muscle-bound man—every inch of him.

I find myself staring for a moment, and when I scan up to his face and see him smiling at me, I cover my eyes.

"Good Goddess," I say. "Put some clothes on."

"Don't have any." He laughs. "Well, I do, but they're kind of shredded right now."

I turn around and wave him back, but he comes up close to me, so close I can close my eyes and let his scent wash over me.

For some reason, that feels wonderful.

"You never need to turn away from me," he whispers in a husky voice.

The sound of it stirs something in me, sending electricity down through my core.

'*Girl, get a grip on yourself,*' I tell myself silently.

"I'd love to grip you," he says.

I turn around again, struggling not to look down. "I didn't say that out loud. How did you hear it?"

"You didn't?" he furrowed his brow.

"I guess it's a mate thing. I heard it too," Braden says.

"What?" I turn around to face him and start to back up again. "What do you mean mate? I'm not old enough to find my mate yet. And I'm sure I don't have a mate!"

"You do. We're your mates."

The way Damon says it stops me in my tracks, and for a moment, I forget about the freezing cold snow blowing all around me.

"That's not possible," I say. "I don't have one mate, much less—" I look around, trying to ignore the fact that Alessandro is still naked. That's really not possible. "Much less three of them. This is ridiculous!"

"Believe me, we're as surprised as you are," Damon says. He nods toward the car. "Alessandro, I have some sweatpants in my pack. You're going to freeze out here."

"Eh, it's not bad." Even so, he heads toward the car, and I feel my eyes staring at his perfectly toned, sculpted ass as he walks past me.

I shake my head. "Look, I don't know what you guys think you know about me, but it's not possible that we can be mates. First of all, there are… too many of you! And I'm not from around here."

"That doesn't matter," Damon says. "We understand that you can't feel it yet, but believe us, we do."

I don't know why he's being so persistent. "I don't have a mate! There's no way the Goddess is doing this to me."

What am I going to do?

I've prayed to the Goddess since I first knew who She was, begging Her not to give me a mate to follow me around and tell me what to do. Now, I've got these three persistent guys doing exactly that. Three of them!

As if on cue, Braden starts in on me. "You'd better come with us. It's freezing out here, and you don't seem to have any provisions."

"Are you kidding me?" I put my hands on my hips. "I'm not some little girl you can chase after and make her come home to you just because you claim I'm your mate. I'm here for a reason. I've had a calling to be here."

"What do you mean?" Damon asks.

"It's the whole reason I'm even here," I say. "I came all the way here because my dreams and the forest called me here. There's a little boy somewhere. Someone needs my help. And I'm not going anywhere with you just because you claim to be my mates. How am I supposed to know whether you are or not? And even if you are, who says I have to accept that? I'm not going to spend the rest of my life with three men coming to my rescue every five minutes!"

They all just sort of stare at me for a few minutes.

"I'm not leaving here," I say firmly. "Mates or whatever, you can just leave and let me go where I need to go. I didn't come all this way to turn back now."

I turn around and start walking away, or at least I am trying to storm off dramatically, but I have to limp a little from the way my ankle twisted.

"Daphne," Damon said softly. "Let us give you a ride."

14

A NEWFOUND TRUST

Ethan

I WAKE up and sit up quickly, my instincts kicking in because I'm in an unfamiliar place. But it's just the resort, Raven pack, and I'm in the room my cousin assigned me for my stay here. I should be out in the forest camp with my warriors, but Cameron insisted that he could handle things there while I spent more time with my family.

There's a reason he's my future Beta.

I lie back down, staring at the ceiling. That was the third night I've dreamed about Rylee. Every time, she's here with me in bed. Her long, raven hair falls over my shoulders as I caress her hips, moving her gently up and down as we find our rhythm. Her eyes meet mine, she moans, and we both let loose at the same time, my vision filled with bright stars that match the silver flakes in her eyes.

Every night there's a similar dream, just a different version of the same amazing connection. The first night, I think it is just my reaction to seeing a beautiful woman. But there's more to the dream than just lust. The way she looks at me is so intense, it feels like our connection comes from deep within our souls.

I wonder if I'm her mate. It's the only thing that makes sense. I guess I'll find out in a few days with my birthday coming up. All of us are due to get our wolves, according to the tests they took long ago. I'm guessing that will change things for my sisters, Matthew, and me forever.

Cameron's voice appears in my mind. 'No movement last night. It's been quiet. We have things packed for your trip back.'

'Thanks,' I say. 'I hate leaving on the eve of battle.'

He chuckles in my head. It's strange how he can do that.

'What?' I ask. 'The rogues are out there, and they might attack any minute.'

'It was a bit dramatic, that's all,' he says. 'The eve of battle.' He laughs again. 'Don't worry. Our warriors are the best. We'll be fine.'

'Well, I also hate that my best friend is missing my birthday party.' I get up and start getting dressed.

'Eh, you know I hate those big shindigs.' He laughs again. 'A few of us guys are going to take you out for drinks and a wolf run when all this is over.'

'Sounds like a plan.'

We disconnect the mind-link, and I've just finished getting dressed when there's a knock on my door. "Come in." I smell her before I see her, the scent of my favorite chocolate mints wafting through the air. "Rylee."

"Alpha Ethan," she says.

"Just Ethan." I won't know for sure that she's my mate for a few days, but I have a feeling I'm right. Calling me by my title hardly seems appropriate, if that's the case.

"Ethan."

The way my name rolls off her tongue gives me a pleasant sensation.

"I hear you're going back to Dark Forest castle," she says.

I nod. "Unfortunately, my birthday is happening, war or not, and my mother would kill me if I didn't show up for it."

She laughs. "I'm starting to want to meet the Luna Queen."

"She will love you." It's hard to stop staring at her beautiful eyes.

"I wanted to talk to you before you left," she says. "And I need to show you something."

"All right."

She gestures for me to follow, and she doesn't even need to because of the way I'm drawn to her. We walk down several hallways until we come to what was once a wing full of smaller hotel rooms. I know that many of the pack members live here.

She looks up and down the hall one more time and unlocks the door. "It's all right. Don't be afraid."

She's not talking to me.

I step into the room and see two children, both so skinny that they're drowning in the borrowed clothes they're wearing. A woman, who looks ill, is sitting up in the bed, and it's obvious that she's been there for a while. She looks at me fearfully.

I put up my hands to show everyone I'm not here to harm them. "It's okay."

Rylee closes the door behind us and locks it.

"I take it this is the lady who needed the bark," I say.

Rylee nods. "This is Amla, my best friend, and her children, Christopher and Maya."

"Pleasure," I say, nodding at all of them. I don't want to go close and shake the woman's hand. She still looks frightened.

"You're big." The little boy comes a little closer to look at me.

I chuckle and squat down to his level. "I'm sure you'll be as big as me when you grow up."

"Nah, you're an Alpha," he says. "I can see that."

"I am, but I have a feeling you could be a great warrior someday," I say.

"He already is."

I turn and face Rylee, and she continues. "They've fought for their lives out there in the forest, controlled by a maniac who craves power. He doesn't care what happens to the people who follow him. I had to bring Amla and the kids here because she was so sick."

I turn to Amla. "You're safe here. I'll make sure you get everything you need, and no one will bother you."

"Do you mean we can go outside and play?" Maya asks.

"Of course," I say. "My cousin is the Alpha here. I have to leave for a while, but he's a kind man, and I'll let him know what's going on here. You'll have food, clothes, and whatever medicine your mom still needs."

"Thank you," Amla says with a weak smile.

"It's no problem," I say. I turn to the kids. "We'll find a suite where you can all have your own beds."

"Yay!" Christopher hollers, then he puts his hand over his mouth.

I chuckle. "No need to be quiet anymore," I say. "Remember, you're safe here."

There's a knock on the door, and I answer it. I've been mind-linking with a few relatives and telling them the whole story, at least, as much of it as I know so far.

"I hear we have some new pack members!" Aunt Kelly says with a smile. "Oh, my, what a handsome young man and beautiful young lady. I have something for you—"

She pulls out a teddy bear for Maya. She takes it cautiously, but it doesn't take long for her to hold it close.

"And for you," Aunt Kelly continues, giving Christopher a set of toy cars.

"Wow, thanks!" He runs over to the corner, sits, and starts playing with them right away.

Isabelle comes in next with the healer, who goes straight to Amla to examine her.

"We've got it from here," Aunt Kelly says.

"Thanks," I say, stepping out of the room to give them some privacy.

Rylee follows me out. "Is there somewhere we can talk?"

I nod. "Come with me."

She follows me to what used to be a small meeting room in the main resort area. We both sit in comfortable chairs.

"That's a wonderful thing you did," she says. "I don't know exactly why I know I can trust you, but I'm pretty sure about it."

"Of course you can," I say. "I'd never hurt women and children, and neither would my cousin or anyone associated with him. You should know that since your sister is his Beta."

She takes a breath. "I wanted to think that, but I've spent too much time listening to the rogue council. They definitely have other ideas. For some reason, once you arrived, everything I was told about the royals just doesn't seem to fit anymore."

"I think I know what you're talking about," I say. "Things feel different to me, too."

She moves a little closer, and I'm suddenly grateful for the wheels on these chairs. "Are we mates, Ethan?"

"I don't know for sure, but I think so," I say. "I don't have my wolf. My siblings and I are getting them in a few days on our twenty-first birthday."

"I got mine on my eighteenth birthday," she says. "But you and your siblings are children of the full moon."

"What's that?"

"You've never heard of that?" she asks. "It's when you don't get your wolf until you're twenty-one. It's said that your wolves will be stronger than usual, more connected to the Moon Goddess. Was your birth on a full moon?"

I shrug. "I don't know, maybe. My mother was a little too preoccupied at the time to check the moon phase." I chuckle a little, and I'm surprised that Rylee joins me. She's become a lot more relaxed in such a short time. I suppose she feels just as comfortable with me as I do with her.

"I guess having four babies at once is quite a feat," she says. "So, you're going home for your birthday party?"

"Yes," I say. "Come with me."

"I can't believe I'm saying this, but okay," she says. "I want to know what's going on between us."

"Me too."

We both scoot in closer, and I can feel her warm breath against my cheek. Her scent is intoxicating, and I lean in to put my lips on hers.

But we don't quite touch before she jumps up. "Um... I need to talk to you before you leave here. There are some things that Alpha Isaac has to know about."

I take a few breaths, still recovering from the almost-kiss.

She looks at me sympathetically, realizing that I need an explanation. "If you're my mate, our first kiss will be when we know that for sure," she says. "It will be my first ever."

I nod. She's never even kissed anyone before. It's hard to pull back and calm down again, but I understand. I want it to be special for her.

We both seemed to realize that we need to get out of the private room before a lot more happens, so we stand and leave, going to meet with Isaac.

When we sit down with him and her sister Katherine, Rylee explains everything. "Calvin is responsible for so much death and suffering. These people don't want war. All they want to do is live peacefully. For most of them, it was a grandfather, or an uncle, or sometimes a grandmother who was initially kicked out of the pack. The generations have survived as rogues ever since because they have nowhere to call home through no fault of their own. They have been told stories about the royals, that they are nothing but selfish people who wish to harm them. It's hard to overcome stories like those when it's all you've ever heard."

"Well, honestly, a lot of the stories were probably true when King Gene was in charge." We all turn to see Aunt Kelly walking in. "He was an asshole, and that's putting it lightly." She looks at Rylee. "Amla and the kids are settled in a nice suite. They'll all have their own rooms and plenty of clothes. They're welcome to eat with us, play outside, and anything else the rest of our pack members do."

"Goddess bless you," Rylee says. She gives Isaac more information about Calvin, his location, and whatever plans she's aware of, and he takes note of it all for handling the oncoming battles, should this Calvin decide to attack a bunch of highly trained warriors.

It sounds like he's stupid enough to do just that.

After lunch, my aunt and cousins wish me a happy birthday and give me a few gifts before Rylee and I get into the car and head out with a small contingent of guards.

I look at the raven-haired beauty next to me and smile. This is going to be a more interesting birthday than I ever imagined.

15

MAYBE A MATE ISN'T SO BAD

Ethan

I normally hate long trips, but this one was a definite exception. Rylee and I talk the whole time as we ride in the SUV. I've never felt so comfortable with a person. There is no subject we can't talk about freely, and her heart is completely free of any judgment.

She tells me about her past. Her parents were happy when my parents decided to make the people at the resort part of the official packs. Things were easier for them after that, and soon they had two daughters. But then they decided to go back to their old pack and see if they were welcome now since the politics had changed. They left their two small daughters behind with friends and hoped they would be welcomed back with open arms.

Unfortunately, nothing changed for Running Creek pack, and they were killed as soon as they entered the pack territory.

"They're one of our more extreme packs," I explain, though I'm sure Rylee already knows that. "I'll go pay them a visit as soon as my birthday is over."

"I'm going with you," she says.

I nod, though something protective seems to awaken in me, and I wonder if that's the right decision. I shake it out of my mind, and we go on to talk about other things.

Eventually, we arrive at the castle. I have to chuckle at all my mom's over-the-top decorations. There are ribbons and banners everywhere, and there are even some ice sculptures in the center of the courtyard. I have no idea how they're not melting.

She's really gone all-out, though I guess this is a special birthday for us.

Of course, Mom is waiting for me as soon as we pull in. She has me wrapped in a hug when I'm barely out the door, but then she pulls back when Rylee steps out.

"And this is...."

"This is Rylee, Mom," I say. "She's the sister of Isaac's Beta, Katherine."

Mom extends her hand, and Rylee shakes it. "Oh, that's wonderful. We've met once, but you were too young to remember."

"We have, Luna Rose?" Rylee asked.

Mom chuckles, looking back and forth at us suspiciously. She seems to have picked up on how well we've been getting along. She's always been very intuitive about those things. "I think that for you, it's just Rose, please." She chuckles, but then gets serious quickly. "I'm so glad you're both here. Your sister, on the other hand, is still off gallivanting who knows where."

"She's not back yet?" I ask.

Mom shakes her head. "No, and we only have one more day, so she'd better get here soon. I hope she doesn't miss your birthday celebration. I want all four of you together."

"Should I go look for her?"

"Oh, goodness, no," she says, shaking her head. "I have an army out looking for her, and I want all my babies to stay here for the next few days."

"We're hardly babies, Mom," I complain.

She looks back and forth at me and Rylee again. "I can see that."

My face turns red, and I hope that Rylee is looking the other way.

Mom clears her throat and is clearly holding back another laugh. "Rylee, why don't we go have a chat and get to know each other?"

"Um, yes, that would be nice."

They walk off together, and Rylee turns around with a confused grin while she follows my mother, the Luna Queen. I'm sure they'll get along fine.

But now, I'm worried about my sister, and I hope she's safe. I can't imagine what kind of people are out there possibly causing trouble for her.

Where is Trisha?

TRISHA

I have to admit, the car is much warmer than walking. The Alphas' scents are nearly overwhelming in such a cramped space—apples and strawberries. It's hard to sit still, really.

It's odd that I have such an attraction to their scent. I wonder if my wolf is awakening since it's so close to my birthday. There's a very strong possibility these guys are my mates, as much as I hate to admit that. But all the signs are there, even though I'm not positive about it yet.

Mom had four mates, so it's not impossible to believe that I have three. But growing up, I never even wanted one. Of course, Mom and my dads were always blissfully in love. They seem to be stronger together and love being around each other. It's not like she ever complained. The more I think about it, the more I start to think that having a mate isn't so bad.

It's just that growing up with four dads, a mom, and two brothers left me a little smothered in the 'caring about me' department. My sister was the only one who just let me vent and didn't try to tell me what to do. I guess I always thought that adding another protector would positively suffocate me.

And now, I have three of them.

Great.

The good thing is, they're all unbelievably hot.

I spend a few minutes just listening to their banter and admiring them.

I have to admit, I was a little disappointed when Alessandro put his clothes back on. Every inch of his body was firm and muscular. I could have stared at that all day. He has some gorgeous blond hair, and those silver eyes are so unique, I could get lost in them.

He's in the back seat, so I can only catch a glimpse of him in the mirror. But every time I do, he smiles.

Braden is also blond, with his hair a little longer like he should be out on the beach somewhere. He has a build more like a runner than a bodybuilder, though he's every bit as muscular as Alessandro. He can be serious at times, but in other moments, I can see his jokester personality come through, especially when he teases the other guys. But it's never mean, and I can tell they have always been good friends. It's harder to see Braden in the mirror, and I don't want to turn around and stare, though I feel like doing just that.

Damon is the intense one. I suppose that comes from being the Alpha King's son. I don't know much about his father other than what I learned in Dark Forest, which I'm quickly learning is probably pretty useless. No one from my kingdom ever spent enough time here to realize that the people here are just like us.

I manage to check out Damon a few times, though I'm trying to be casual about it. His jet-black hair shimmers in the light. His ocean blue eyes are looking straight ahead at the road as he drives. He seems to be the kind of guy who notices everything. He's always alert as though something might jump out at us at any minute, and he'll have to be ready to shift and deal with it.

I suppose that's possible. They did say this place is dangerous, but I'm not sure why.

I'm starting to realize how much safer I am with these three around. Though I don't feel the mate bond completely yet, I feel so comfortable riding in this car with them as though I've known them forever. I have to admit; it's a good feeling.

It's too bad I have no idea where we're going.

"Guys," I say.

Everyone stops talking and looks at me, except for Damon, who gives me sideways glances in between watching the road.

No one says anything, so I guess they're waiting for me. "Um, I really don't know where we're going."

I feel the car slowing down, and Damon pulls off to the side of the road and stops. He turns and looks at me. "You know, it didn't occur to me to ask."

Braden starts laughing in the back seat. "Wow, you know things just got real when the future Alpha King forgets to ask where he's going."

"Hey, you didn't ask her, either," Damon counters.

"True. But I've never ridden in a car with my mate before," Braden says.

"Well, neither have I," Damon says. He turns around and looks at him and Alessandro. "The one who has been around her the most took a ship from Dark Forest."

Braden turns and looks at Alessandro, too. "Yeah. You were used to being around her. Why didn't you ask her where she was going?"

"*She,*" I interrupt, "is sitting right here. Maybe we should spend just a little more time getting to know one another. I think I should explain what I'm doing here."

They all went quiet again, and I don't know whether to cry from happiness or just laugh. Back at my castle, if I tried to talk, either a brother or a father would break in and start telling me what I was supposed to do or how I was supposed to feel or what I really meant by what I didn't get to say.

So, this is what it's like to have mates. I have someone who listens to me... three of them.

This is different.

"Before I even left home, I would get these visions," I explain. "The only person I ever told was my sister. She was the only one who took the time to listen. Anyway, I have dreams. At first, they were really vague. I just had this feeling that someone needed me for something, but none of the images were clear. After a while, I started to see a little boy by a village."

They are all still quiet and listening, so I continue. "Then I started to feel different when I was out in the forest. It's like a spirit gives me messages. That's the only way I can explain it. I have to be in nature, touching the trees, the ground, being in some sort of contact with nature. Then, it guides me. So, I can't exactly get a bead on where I'm going in a car."

"Does it have to be a forest?" Damon asked. "It's a bit barren out here, but I know there are forests as we head to the mountains."

I shrugged. "I guess so. I wasn't really feeling anything walking down the road."

They all look at each other with wide eyes. "What's wrong?" I ask.

"We'll take you there," Alessandro says. "But the forest here… they say it's haunted."

16

NORTHSIDE MOUNTAIN

Damon

I'm not crazy about driving the woman who I'm sure is my mate toward one of the most dangerous places in the kingdom, but I'm doing it anyway because that's what she wants. I'm not really used to being this way. I can usually order people to stay away from things that are dangerous like this.

It's odd that I can't be that way with my mate. I want to protect her from danger with every fiber of my being, but part of what I admire most about her is her strength and determination. Because of that, I'm extremely averse to doing or saying anything that might crush that aspect of her.

Well, that's something new. I guess I'll just have to get used to it.

I'm pretty sure that Alessandro and Braden feel the same way because they haven't said anything that would stop us from going, either. I guess as long as we're with her, there's no way anyone can hurt her.

We've long passed the part of Northside where I've been before. I don't like coming up here, so normally, I don't. Ironically, the last time I was here was when Alessandro, Braden, and I were teenagers.

The three of us and a van load of other friends came up here on a dare. We made it to the base of the mountain then turned back before our parents caught wind of our stupid idea.

Now, we're heading up the road going up the mountain, and we're increasing in altitude fast. The sun set a while ago, so it's dark and hard to see anything outside the headlights.

"How weird that it's not snowing," Alessandro says. "There isn't even any accumulated snow. You'd think that there would be."

"Yeah, I always thought this whole place was buried in it," I agree. "I guess not."

"I'm surprised that there's even a road here," Braden says. "I didn't see it that one time we came here when we were kids."

I nod. I've been thinking the same thing myself, though it doesn't seem like anyone has maintained it at all. "Me, neither. It's fairly rough. It must be really old."

"No one ever talks about this place anymore, so I'm not sure how long ago it was that people were here building roads," Alessandro adds. "It's strange that they'd do that for no real reason, though. All the old folks I know say no one ever comes here, so why a road?"

"Well, someone must have built this for some reason," Daphne says.

She hasn't spoken in a while, and it makes me glance over at her for a second. It's hard to see her in the dark, but her eyes have a little shimmer to them.

I turn back to focus on the road before I get lost in those eyes.

We soon come to a place where it's so bad that I can't keep driving, not in this car. The road runs along the side of a mountain, and its outer edges are so eroded that it's just not safe to pass in a vehicle this wide.

"Here's where we get out, I guess," I say.

Exiting the car, it's surprising how quiet it is outside. The forest edge is just against the road, yet I don't hear any of the sounds I expect to hear—no crickets, no frogs. I don't sense any creatures nearby at all.

"Are you all getting that empty feeling?" Alessandro asks.

I nod. "It's like this forest is deserted, but that can't be."

"What do you mean?" Daphne asks.

I turned to her. "I forgot that you don't have your wolf. We can't sense any animals around here at all."

"I guess it is pretty quiet," she says. "Which way do we go now?"

"That's your call," Braden says. "How is it that you hear whatever it is telling you where to go?"

"I just need to be in nature like this, focused, with my eyes closed," she explains. "I'll lean against this tree."

"All right. We'll keep watch," I say.

We all wait a few minutes, watching her lean against the tree and close her eyes. She looks so beautiful in the moonlight. The smile that lights up her face is gone, but there's a different kind of beauty in this serious, thoughtful expression that fascinates me. I can't take my eyes off her.

After a few minutes, she opens her eyes. "Well, that was strange. It told me to follow the brightest star."

We all look up. We're still close enough to the road that the sky isn't lost in the forest canopy. Sure enough, there's one very big, very bright star in the northeast. I'm certainly not one to follow stars or believe it when someone says they're being led by spirits somewhere, but now, I don't even question Daphne. I just think of all this as a mission, something I have to help her do.

I guess that's more of the mate bond in play.

We figure out the best way to head in that direction, which happens to be straight into the forest rather than down what's left of the road. The guys and I grab what we can of the provisions we've packed in the car and start heading in.

It would be a lot faster if we all shifted, I know, but Daphne can't do that yet, so it's best to stay in human form and stay close. We walk for a while until I hear a loud yell from behind.

"Argh!"

We whirl around to see Alessandro as he catches himself with his palms on the ground and pushes himself back up.

"What the hell, Alessandro?" Braden hollers. "Watch the forest, not... never mind."

Alessandro shoots him a glare but then shrugs. "What?"

I'd seen the tree root protruding, but I had the sense to avoid it. Being behind Daphne, I guess he was enjoying the view.

Braden shakes his head and we all turn back around. I catch a glimpse of Daphne snickering as she starts walking.

It's still quiet for quite a distance until we get deep into the forest where we all smell smoke. Daphne tells us that she thinks we should go toward it, so we do. I'm still not used to following someone else's dreams, but this seems like the most natural thing in the world to do.

Eventually, we find the campfire. It's in a clearing with logs arranged around it for seating. There's a grate on the fire with a steaming pot on it, and an old man stirring it looks up as we approach.

"Who's there?" the man calls out.

I step forward and notice two elderly men. Northside is part of my kingdom, and I'll inherit the throne to this kingdom soon, so these people are my subjects, whoever they are. I might as well find out who's hanging out up here in this part of my kingdom.

"I'm Alpha King Heir Damon Barlowe," I say. "These are my friends and my mate. And you are?"

Daphne furrows her brow slightly at my introduction, but she says nothing.

They both stand and show me the sign of respect, not something I'm expecting in what is supposed to be the roughest place in my kingdom.

"Alpha Heir, it's a pleasure to meet you," the same man says. "I am Edor, and this is my brother, Easton." His brother gives a nod.

"Why are you here in this cold and abandoned part of the kingdom?" I ask. "And why is this forest devoid of animals?"

"And why is there no snow here?" Alessandro adds.

"I'm happy to explain." Edor gestures toward the campfire, and we all sit around it. I pull up one of the log seats so Daphne doesn't have to sit on the ground.

Once we are all seated, he begins. "My brother and I were part of the crew who built the roads here back when we were young. It was beautiful here. It still is. The idea was to build a resort for the royal family and visiting dignitaries. Was going to be a beautiful place, fancy, with all the trimmings."

No one has ever told me that our family had ever planned to build a resort.

"But the throne changed hands to the Barlowes, and the idea was scrapped." He looks at me. "That would have been your great-grandfather who took the throne, I believe."

So, it wasn't even my family. It must have been the Wilcox family, who ruled before us. "How old are you two?" I ask.

He chuckles. "Old enough."

"So why didn't you leave when they stopped plans to build the resort?" Daphne asks.

"We did," Easton chimes in. "We went home just like nothing had ever happened. But then we started to get sick and got weaker and weaker. We came back here figuring there was no prettier place to die than up on this mountain. But as soon as we ate those berries over there—" He gestures toward a bush off to the side. "Those made all the pain go away. We tried bringing some off the mountain, but they only work when you stay here. So, we figured it's better to stick around and feel great than to die miserably down south."

"We figure it was the reason for the resort," Edor says. "They must have found out that they only work up here and decided it wasn't worth it. I guess it's not a good idea for a king to be stuck on a mountain. Plus, we think that eating these and then leaving the mountain made us sick in the first place."

"Probably," I agreed.

"Last I heard, the Wilcox family went across the ocean and built a resort up in the woods somewhere there in Dark Forest," Edor continues.

Daphne's eyes go wide at that revelation, though I don't know why. She turns away for a few seconds, and when she looks back, her expression is neutral again. I decide to ask about that later when we're alone.

"I don't know what happened to that idea," Edor adds.

We talk to the brothers for a couple of hours, learning a lot about Northside. It isn't at all what I expected.

"We've always been told that Northside is full of nothing but criminals," Braden says after a while. "The rumor is that this is where outlaws come to hide.

"Eventually, Alpha King Wilcox ordered that no one was to return here," Edor explained. "So, I suppose you would call us outlaws. Maybe that's how the rumors started."

"I suppose so," I agree.

Daphne stands. "Gentlemen, I'm afraid I need to step over there for a moment." She lowers her voice to a whisper beside me. "I have to pee."

"Oh," I say. I stand to follow her, but she puts her hand on my arm, and pleasurable sparks of electricity radiate down it. I can't tell whether Daphne feels it, but maybe not since she's still without her wolf.

"I can handle this myself," she says, chuckling a little.

"Daphne, I can't let you go out away from the campfire alone," I insist.

That just makes her laugh more. "I forgot you guys were still calling me Daphne."

"Why wouldn't we?" Alessandro asked.

She shook her head. "That's not my name."

"Well, what is it?" I ask, surprised.

She chuckles again. "I'll tell you when I get back. I kind of need to go take care of this right now. I'm only going to be a few yards that way."

I don't like it, but she can't take care of business in front of these old men, and she doesn't know for sure that we're her mates yet, so I can't refuse to give her the privacy.

"Holler if you need us," I say.

"Of course." She smiles and heads into the forest.

It's so dark that I can't see her, but I still hear her movements, and that's reassuring.

But after a few moments, she screams.

I run over there, along with Alessandro and Braden, who are both as shaken as I am.

She's nowhere to be seen.

17

THE BIRTHDAY PARTY

Ethan

"Any word?" Mom looks so panicked as she asks my dads if anyone has found Trisha yet.

I'm so mad at that girl. My sister likes to wander, and there's nothing wrong with that in my opinion, until she's not showing up for our birthday party when Mom has worked so hard to make it perfect. Not just that, but since no one knows where she is, Mom is worried, and it's not cool to make her worry right now, especially in front of all these people who have come to the party. The room is positively packed.

But my dads are on the case, soothing Mom and reassuring her that Trisha is fine.

"She'll be okay, little flower," one of my dads, Tristan, Trisha's biological father, says. Little flower has always been Mom's pet name with him. I suppose that makes sense since her name is Rose.

I have a feeling that Trisha is okay. Even though all have different fathers, my siblings, and I have agreed that we feel a connection to each other, probably because we shared the womb. It might have to do with what Rylee said as well, that we were children of the full moon. Maybe there's something going on with the Moon Goddess there, like She's always guiding us.

I just feel like I would know if there was something wrong with Trisha, though I can't know that for sure.

But my mind is off Trisha soon as I think of Rylee, which makes me smile. I woke up pretty sure that I am her mate since she was the last thing I dreamed about last night and the most prominent thing on my mind all day. Rylee is pretty sure of it too, which is why she insisted on coming late to the party. She wants me to enjoy time with my family, especially after all my mom's preparations, before we feel the mate bond. I guess after that, I won't be much interested in parties and birthday cake.

I left my dads to handle Mom and head over to the main table, where Matthew is looking around.

"Lose someone?" I ask, chuckling.

"You know I'm looking for my mate," he says. "And I don't see her. That's not fair. You have Rylee already."

I shrug. "I don't know for sure she's my mate yet, but I'm pretty sure. I know you'll find yours soon. Don't worry."

"Easy for you to say," he says.

"I don't see mine, either," Reeva says. "I guess we both just need to wait."

"So unfair," Matthew says again, shaking his head.

We turn as Mom and the dads walk up onto the stage. Mom approaches the microphone, and the room goes silent.

"Thank you, everyone, for being here tonight," she says. "I couldn't be happier that my four babies are turning twenty-one. This is such a special night for our family, and I thank you all for joining us to share in it."

She nods toward the main table, which is a long one because it's filled with aunts, uncles, and cousins, and Chief Beta Adam and his wife Shelby, who are pretty much my uncle and aunt. Isaac and Isabelle have stayed back at their pack to bring the rogue situation under control. It's not the greatest time for her to travel anyway since the baby could come any moment.

Mom continues her speech, and we all get up one by one to say a few words. Mostly I just thank everyone for coming. The only part of this party I'm excited about is seeing Rylee. It's pretty hard to be patient, but she said she would wait for midnight. It can't come soon enough.

We eat a huge feast, enjoy some cake for dessert, and Mom even makes me, Reeva, and Matthew blow out candles on the cake, which I can tell she loves to see. I guess she'll never stop being the mom of four Alpha's babies, no matter how old we get. I love my mom, so it's fine by me if I have to do a few silly things once in a while for her sake.

Everyone starts dancing eventually, and there is only one woman I want to dance with. My sister and brother take turns dancing with whoever asks them, but I don't really feel up to it and just send all the ladies over to my brother. None of them seem to mind.

Finally, it's midnight. I've been staring at the door waiting for her when it opens. Rylee stands there with a smile, the most beautiful creature I'd ever seen. It's like she sparkles for only me to see, though I know she's captured quite a few eyes with her entrance.

She's wearing a silky, strapless, deep blue dress, the same color as her eyes, with black accents that make her jet-black hair look even darker. From this distance I can't see the flecks of silver in her eyes that I love so much, but I can see them sparkle in the chandelier light.

She walks straight up toward me, never taking her eyes off me and smiling beautifully when I reach out my hand to her.

It feels like electricity fires up my nerves at our first touch, and I can tell that she feels it too. I lead her straight to the dance floor and pull her close to me, swaying softly to the music. It's like everyone disappears except her, and all I want to do is hold her close.

But the more I hold her like that, the more I get other ideas about what I want to do with her. All the dreams I've had about her flash through my mind, and it feels like forever before people start piling out of the ballroom. I have to force myself to pull away from my dance with Rylee just long enough to thank people and say goodbye, but I go right on dancing with her as soon as I can.

She is still in my arms when the servants start clearing away all the tables.

"Time for some privacy," I whisper into her ear.

She nods with a smile, and I take her hand, leading her up the stairs to my room. When I pull her inside, I gently push her up against the door as I lock it. I reach my hand up to her cheek, using every ounce of energy I have to keep from crushing her lips against mine. This is her first kiss, and if it kills me, it's going to be special for her.

I caress that beautiful cheek for a while before softly touching her lips to mine. She moans in response and wraps her arms around me, and I deepen the kiss. She becomes the air I breathe at this moment. I taste her delicious tongue with mine, running my fingers through her hair and savoring the feeling.

I can't hold back anymore. My hands roam along her body, feeling every inch of her until I reach her hips, which I grasp tightly and pull up, cradling her butt with my hands as I carry her over to my bed.

She giggles as I plop her down on it, and I gaze into those beautiful blue eyes, my whole soul feeling ecstasy with her mere presence. I don't want to tear that lovely dress—I want her to keep it forever as a memory of this night when we recognized our mate bond—but it's hard to control my hands as I undo the zipper and expose her bare skin.

My hands on her body feel even better without the cloth covering it. That spark I felt with her first touch multiplies a thousand times as I run my hands over her, feeling every inch of her delicious body. I'm just wondering how long I should wait to take the next step when she starts to pull at my clothes. I chuckle as I help her remove them as quickly as we can.

Gently, I pull her legs apart, and she widens them further, her silver-sparkle eyes meeting mine as I move on top of her. Knowing it was her first kiss, I know that of course she's also a virgin, and I don't want to hurt her, so I hesitate.

"You can't hurt me," she whispers as if knowing my thoughts. "I want you, Ethan."

That's all the reassurance I need before I feel her wet opening with my fingers before I bring my stiff cock to her and gently slide in. Despite what she's just said, I give her some time, working it in slowly. She gasps a little at one part, and I stop for a moment before she nods, and I slide my dick all the way inside her, feeling her tight, wet walls squeeze against every inch of me.

Once inside, she shows no evidence of pain. In fact, she rocks her hips back to meet mine until we're in a fast, almost panicked rhythm. With every stroke, that electric tingling rides up my entire body, and I can't help moaning with pleasure.

There's no greater feeling than being inside my mate, calling out her name, and I don't care whether half the castle can hear me. It doesn't take long before I feel her tighten up even more, as if that is even possible, and her rhythm changes.

Her eyes roll back a little then meet mine again as she lets out a final moan of pleasure, pushing against me and squeezing so hard that I feel myself reaching my peak. With a final few desperate strokes, I pound inside her, feeling her juices explode just as mine do as I push as hard as I can to get to her core.

I'm still inside her as I collapse, careful not to fall too heavily on top of her but so spent I can't move any farther. We're both sweating, our hearts pounding against each other and our breathing so fast it seems like we've run a marathon.

Slowly, we both calm our breaths, still in unison along with our heartbeats, which slow to match each other's soft rhythm. It's only then that I have the strength to roll off her, pulling her toward me so her head is against my chest.

I gently stroke her beautiful black hair as it shimmers in the moonlight streaming through the curtains.

I have found my mate, and I will never leave her.

1 8

WHAT'S HER NAME?

Ethan

I WAKE up to the sound of giggling and roll over with a smile on my face, bringing Rylee into my arms. This is going to be our life from now on, and seeing the twinkle in her eyes makes me realize how lucky I am.

"What's so funny?" I ask, pulling her in for a kiss so she doesn't even have the chance to answer.

But she giggles against my mouth and pulls back, and I don't even get my kiss. "I'm sorry. This is just so…. Do you realize how much I hated royals? And now I'm in a castle in bed with a prince."

"Well, I don't see what's so funny about that," I say teasingly, stealing that kiss from her. "And I'm not just any prince, you know," I add when we come up for air. "I'm your mate."

"That's what's so funny about it." She settles her head against my chest, tracing the lines of my muscles. "I don't mean to laugh. I'm just happy. And I never expected things to go this way."

"Well, your sister is a Beta. You've been around a lot of royalty."

"I suppose so, but I never thought of Isaac that way," she explains.

107

"He's an Alpha, but it wasn't like we were in a palace, though it is a fancy place. I just… I felt more connected to the people in the forest, and they don't have a king."

"They kind of do." I run my fingers through her jet-black hair. "Calvin is in charge, and he probably lives a lot better than any of the people he was ruling over."

"I'll say." She moves suddenly, propping up her head with her elbow. "He actually had children erect his tents, and then he'd send them off for the night to sleep in the forest."

"So, there you go," I say. "He's the kind of 'royalty' you should be hating."

"I know that now." She kisses me and pulls back again. "I don't know how I was so wrong."

"That doesn't matter now." I grab her and pull her on top of me, and she giggles again. "What matters now is planning our wedding. My mother is going to be so excited."

"I hope she likes me," she says.

"She'll love you," I assure her. "And speaking of Mother, she's in my head right now asking where I'm at."

"Are you supposed to be somewhere?"

"Yes, apparently there's a whole post-birthday breakfast going on in a half an hour," I say.

She gives me a quick peck on the lips then climbs off me, scooting off the bed. "Well, are you coming? I don't want to piss off the Luna Queen."

I laugh. "She could never be mad at you. But I can't wait to tell her about us."

"I'm pretty sure she knows, as does the rest of the kingdom. We weren't very discreet about it."

I laugh, standing up. "I suppose not."

We hurry to get cleaned up and dressed then head downstairs hand-in-hand. We don't get far before Mom and Aunt Kelly come running up to us.

"Oh, my goodness!" Mom practically squeals. "My baby boy has found his mate!"

"Mom, I—"

"And you're so beautiful!" she continues, ignoring me. "Isn't she beautiful, Kelly?"

"Stunning," Kelly agrees. "That hair is going to be a knockout in your wedding dress."

"I—" Rylee gets one word out before Mom continues.

"Oh, the wedding dress!" she says, now almost with a screech to her voice, she's so excited.

She takes Rylee's hand and pretty much pulls her away from me, and Aunt Kelly falls in on the other side of her while they walk her toward the breakfast hall, still chattering on about weddings. Rylee manages to get a quick wave in toward me. At least she's laughing.

"Wow."

I turn to see my brother Matthew standing with his arms crossed. "That makes me almost hope I don't have a mate."

"I hope she's okay," I say.

"I wouldn't worry." He shakes his head. "Your mate seems like she can hold her own against our crazy relatives."

"I hope so."

"By the way, congratulations, little brother," he says. I shake my head because he was born only a few minutes before me, so I'm technically younger, I guess. He likes to remind me of that for some reason.

I ignore it. "Thanks. I'm sure you'll find your mate soon and Reeva as well."

He shrugs. "Doesn't bother me. I can wait. But right now, I smell food."

We both laugh and head to the breakfast hall where my mom, Kelly, and now my honorary aunt Shelby still have Rylee trapped. But she looks like she's having a good time, so I don't try to rescue her. They do need to make those wedding arrangements anyway. I want to be married to her as soon as I can.

Finally, we all sit, and I'm next to my mate again. "Are you all right?"

She laughs. "I'm fine. Your family is really nice."

"I'm glad," I say. "My mom can be overwhelming when she's excited. I'm the first of us to find my mate, so you're probably getting the worst of it."

She laughs again and gives me a light kiss. "If that's the worst she has to offer, I'll take it. I like your mom."

"I'm glad."

We have a great breakfast, and Mom and the dads give some speeches to the crowd in attendance, which isn't much smaller than the celebration last night.

"I'm just so happy that my little baby boy has found his mate," my mother says.

I can feel my cheeks turning red. For some reason, that comes easy for me, and there's no way I can turn it off. If I try, they just get redder.

She's about to say more when the double doors burst open and some warriors run in. All four of my dads stand instantly as the warriors run up to our head table and give the sign of respect.

"Forgive our intrusion on your celebration," the highest ranking man says. "There's urgent news from the royal city. The marketplace has been attacked by rogues, and we have multiple casualties."

Mom gasps, and worry crosses over her face. Rylee and I both stand and run around the table toward the warriors.

"Dispatch the first battalion," my dad Tristan says.

"Already done, Your Majesty."

My biological father, Eli, speaks up. "I'll go take charge of things." He gives my mother a kiss on the cheek and tells his Beta to get his car ready.

"I'm going with you," I say, stepping forward.

"And I'm going with you."

I turn to see Rylee beside me with a determined look on her face.

"I can't let you—"

She holds up her hand to stop me before I can say any more. "I'm trained. I'm a warrior. And I'm going with you. After all, stirring up the rogues was my fault."

Alessandro

My heart feels like it's falling out of my chest, seeing the empty forest ahead of us. "Where is she?" Damon asks.

"I don't know, but we're going to find her," I say before shifting.

It doesn't take long to catch her scent, and I see the others have done so as well since we're all running in the same direction. But it doesn't take long before her scent just drops off.

We shift back, and their faces look the same as I feel.

"What the hell?" Braden asks. "There's no road here, no cars. Her scent couldn't have disappeared like that."

"Agreed," I say. "Let's backtrack and see if we missed anything."

We all shift again and go back the way we came then forward again, and both times the scent stops abruptly in the same spot.

'Let's go back, get our stuff, and regroup,' Damon says in the mind-link. I'm glad we can talk to each other that way as Alphas because it makes it so much easier to coordinate things.

We head back to the campsite and shift back, throwing on some clothes from our backpacks. Edor runs up to us.

"What happened?" he asks.

Out of nowhere, Braden grabs him by the shirt and drags him backward toward a tree. Luckily, he holds off before slamming the old man into it. "Where is she? What kind of fucked up magic do you have in this forest?"

Edor holds up his hands in surrender. "I swear, it's not me. The only magic I know about is the berries. What happened to the young lady?"

"Her scent just disappeared in the middle of nowhere," Damon explains, prying Braden's fingers off the man.

I understand how Braden feels. The pain of having Daphne missing is like having a sledgehammer pound right on my chest.

"I swear, we don't know how that could happen," Easton says, also holding his hands up in a surrender pose. "But there are some strange things that happen up here sometimes. We didn't have anything to do with it, though, and we hope the young lady is okay."

Braden drops back and leans against a tree. I can see that he feels the same way I do.

"We'll just need to make a guess as to which way they—whoever they are—took her and just head that way." He looks at the two old men. "Are there any towns nearby where they might take her?"

Edor shakes his head. "There's nothing up here since we never built the resort. This is pretty much the top of the mountain. The only thing that comes close to a town is back down in the flatlands."

Easton nods. "Back down the road it'll veer off to the east. A few people made a settlement there. That's the only place we know of where there are people around."

We practically run back to the car with as many supplies as we can quickly grab from the campsite, and Damon jumps into the driver's seat while we get in back. He backs the car down the road as far as he needs to until the road is wide enough to turn around, then he floors it down the mountain.

"What if they were lying?" Braden asks.

"The old men? I don't think they were," I say. "They seem pretty straightforward."

"I guess." Braden taps his fingers on the window impatiently, though Damon is driving as fast as the car and the road will allow. It's not fast enough for me, either.

"I wonder what her name is," Braden says.

"What?"

"Just before she left, remember? She said her name isn't Daphne."

In all the rush, I've forgotten about that. "Maybe that's why people are after her. Do you think?"

"That's possible," Damon says.

"I hope we find her soon," I say. She has to be okay. She just can't be hurt–or worse–not when I haven't even had the chance to learn her real name.

19

CAPTIVE

There are about five guys dragging me along, or at least, they're trying to. I'm kicking, thrashing around, and trying to grab hold of branches as they pass them, but I don't get my grip on anything for very long before one of the guys pries my hand loose, and they move on quickly.

Screaming is out of the question now because my mouth is bound up tight, though I got off a bit of a shriek back where they first grabbed me, so I hope all my Alphas heard that and are catching up with these creeps.

In the next second, they're wrapping something around my eyes, and then instantly, I feel myself drop to the ground. In that same moment, my arms are free, and I whip them around to try to grab one of the men, but there's nobody. I reach up and tear off the cloth against my eyes. I can't see clearly at first, but it's obvious that there are bars in front of me.

How am I in a dungeon cell when I was just in the middle of the forest two seconds ago?

I feel groggy, like I've been drugged or something, but there wasn't time for that, was there? I hear a voice not far from me, a woman, though I can't see her.

"Excellent work," she says.

"Should we go ahead and finish her off?"

It's a man's voice, low and gruff, and it makes a fearful shudder run up my spine.

"Not yet," the woman says. "I need to locate the wolf statue, and I have a feeling she knows where it is."

My wolf statue?

"But I promise, I'll let you do the honor when the time comes. For now, just leave her."

Then it goes pitch black, and I hear their footsteps walk away. I stand up and feel my way toward the front bars. "No! Don't leave me here! Who are you, and what do you want with me?"

But my voice just echoes in the darkness.

I close my eyes and try to reach someone, anyone, in the mind-link. I know I'm way too far away with my family and my pack all the way in Green Mountain, but I have to do something. Of course, no one answers, and I slump back against the wall.

I think about the Alphas. I know they chased these people, but some kind of magic took me from the forest to this place, so I doubt they can find me. I know they're my mates now. I felt it at midnight when I turned twenty-one, though I didn't tell them about it. I'd known they were my mates before really, but once my birthday hit, it was so intense. I was pulled to them like a strong magnet, all three of them. My mother had four mates. I guess it makes sense that I have three. They seem to be okay with it. I think we'll be happy... if I ever get out of here.

I haven't had a chance to shift yet. I wonder if I ever will, or if this woman will tell them to kill me before I get a chance to live a real life.

I wonder why I can't reach my mates in the mind-link. We should be able to communicate, I think. I'm pretty sure we're in the same forest or at least still in Northside, so they can't be too far away, even though we haven't had a chance to use it with each other yet. Apparently, something in the cell is blocking it.

Leaning against the wall still, I keep thinking about my three mates and try to stay still, saving my strength for the first opportunity to escape. A guard passes with the beam of his flashlight moving back and forth. I stand and run to the cell bars.

"Hey, let me out of here," I say. "I know a lot of important people who can give you a huge reward."

He laughs. "That's what they all say. If I had a penny for everyone who said I'd get a reward from the people they knew back home, I wouldn't even need a reward." He snickers, apparently pleased at his observation.

"But with me, it's real," I say. I stop short of telling him that I'm a Dark Forest princess. I'm not sure who these people are or what they want with me, but I know things might be worse if they know I'm royalty and can fetch a high reward. And for all I know, they might hate Dark Forest and kill me just to teach the royal family over there a lesson. So, I can't say much that will really convince the guy of anything.

He laughs again and walks on, swinging his flashlight. I stare at the lit bits of wall that I can see as he does that, trying to see what kind of place this is. But he's soon gone, and with him, any last trace of light.

I feel my way to the side wall and slide down it, sitting on the floor and leaning against it. Even though this whole place is dark, something about being by the outer wall of the cell is comforting.

I close my eyes and think about the Alphas again. I wish I had let one of them come stand guard when I walked away from the campfire.

Somehow, I manage to get to sleep, and I wake up with a start when the lights come on again. I see a shadow approaching and blink my eyes to clear my vision.

A little boy steps in front of my cell with a tray of food, and I jump up. "It's you!"

I think I've scared him because he steps back with wide eyes.

"No, I'm sorry," I say softly, waving my hands. "I didn't meet to scare you. I just…. I know you from somewhere, okay?"

He reluctantly steps forward again, opening something in the cell door that allows him to slide the tray in, then he closes it again. He gets up and starts to walk away.

"No, wait," I say. "Please?"

He hesitates, then turns around again.

My eyes have adjusted to the light now, and I'm positive about what I'm seeing now.

It's the little boy from my dream.

His clothes are ratty, and he's barefoot, his face covered in dirt, the same way he always looks in my dream. I'm suddenly not as panicked or even angry that they've kidnapped me because I've found him, the boy who needed me. I'm right where I was supposed to be.

Now, I need to decide how I can help him. The steel bars around me don't make it easy.

"What's your name?" I ask.

He bites his bottom lip like he's not sure he's supposed to answer. But after a few moments, his quiet voice says, "Aryx."

"Aryx," I repeat. "That's a nice name."

He shrugs.

"Do you live in a village near here?" I ask.

He nods.

"Are your parents there?"

This time, he shakes his head. I take a light breath and step a little closer. At first, he seems to want to step away, but he stays there as I approach.

"Where are your parents?" I ask.

He shrugs again. "Coraline says I don't need them."

"Who is Coraline?" I ask.

"She does magic," he says. "Says I have to do what she says."

"It doesn't sound like she's a nice person, telling you that you don't need your parents and you have to do as she says," I say. "Are you afraid of her?"

He doesn't answer, and it doesn't matter. I already know.

"It's okay to be afraid. I'm going to help."

I can see a glimmer of hope in his eyes.

"Aryx, I need to get to your village," I say. "I know you don't know me, but I've come here to help you and the people living in your village. Do you think that you could find the key to this cell for me so I can come help you?"

Alpha King Rohan

"Kurt!" I scream it pretty loudly because I don't have any idea where the fuck that man is. He should always be close enough to serve me, especially during wartime. I hold my head, which hurts, and take another sip of my tea. I'm glad Coraline gave me such a big supply of it this time. It's the only thing that seems to keep my head from aching.

"Rohan, I'm right here," he says.

The insolent fool. "That's 'Your Majesty' to you!" I bellow. Why doesn't this man address me by my proper title? It's not like I haven't reminded him a thousand times.

"Your Majesty," he says, rolling his eyes. "You don't need to scream. You can call me in the mind-link."

"Oh." I take a sip of tea. At first, this stuff tasted like crap, sort of like dirty socks, though I'd never actually eaten soiled socks. But after some time it grew on me, and now, I feel like I need to drink it all the time. I guess it still tastes like socks though. I've just developed a taste for footwear, I guess.

"Did you need something?" he asks.

"What? Oh. Yes. I need the report from the battlefield," I say.

"We have no reports yet… Your Majesty." There he goes, rolling his eyes again.

"What do you mean? We don't have a report?" I chug down the rest of my tea. The headache is starting to pound harder.

"We're waiting for the messenger ship," he says. "Remember? We assigned ships to travel along with the armies that would bring back news at different intervals."

"Well, this is an interval, isn't it?" I start to raise my voice again because my Beta is annoying me. He's good at that.

"It is… Your Majesty. But they only passed that checkpoint yesterday. They've gotten the message from the general, but it will take some time for that ship to make it back."

"Well, that's ridiculous," I say. "Can't they just fly it back?"

"Your Majesty has outlawed air travel," he says with a sigh.

"Oh." I suppose I did do that. Coraline said it would cut down on miscreants from Dark Forest coming here. She really does hate that place. She's told me that she doesn't want anyone from there to step foot in Green Mountain. I'm inclined to agree. I don't remember why, but I agree. Yes, that's right.

"Um… Rohan?"

"What?"

"Are you feeling all right?" he asks. "Lately you seem like you're spacing out."

"What? I'm the king! How dare you accuse me of being—" I forget where I was going with that.

"Um, yeah," he says. "That's what I'm talking about."

"You aren't making any sense," I say. "Get out of there and go find someone who makes sense and bring them back here!"

He sighs, and rolls his eyes, which he does a lot lately, and just walks out of the room. Good riddance. I'll find someone to talk to who knows how to speak to a king.

But in the meantime, maybe I'll have another cup of tea.

2 0

THE HIDDEN SORCERESS

Ethan

Chaos is the only word to describe it as we arrive at the marketplace. It's normally a happy place, set up with vendors on both sides of the street with families coming to buy goods and produce, and there are usually quite a few food trucks there making street tacos and things like that.

But right now, it's a mess, worse than a regular battlefield because there are women and children here, innocent people who are just trying to have a normal day. Dad's Beta already has the battalion here, but since the rogues are so disorganized, the warriors are chasing them around everywhere picking them off one by one.

Rylee steps out of the car before it rolls to a stop, and I'm right behind her.

"I'll get these women out of here," she says.

I don't even have time to kiss her or say a word before she's gone, scooping up a little girl and running with her mother toward cover. I've never been so worried and impressed at the same time. I don't want her anywhere near the rogues, but there she is in the thick of it.

And she's running up to women and guiding them off to safety without hesitating.

I have no idea how to process these feelings, but I don't have time to right now anyway because I catch sight of a pair of rogues leaping toward a fruit stand. With my focus on Rylee and our lovemaking for the past twenty-four hours, I haven't had time to even shift for the first time. But that doesn't seem to matter to my wolf because the minute I see those people in danger, I feel myself shift mid-air as I run over to them, my jaw landing right on one of the wolves' necks. I make short work of him, and the other one's eyes go wide as he tries to run away, but one of Dad's soldiers takes care of him when he runs right in his path.

I finally have a moment to see Matthew, and I can't believe the size difference between his wolf and the rest of our warriors. He's huge. I guess there's some truth to that born on the full moon bit.

It doesn't take long before all the rogues are either killed or arrested and loaded into prisoner vans. I shift back surprisingly easily and one of the support troops hands me a pair of sweats right away.

"Well, that was different," Matthew says as he walks up to me. "You were huge, man."

I laugh. "So were you. I think that brown wolf just about pissed himself when he saw you coming."

"I guess I don't need to worry about you boys," Dad says, coming up behind us. "Good work."

I nod and look around. The place really is a mess, and I wish these people hadn't had to take the brunt of the attacks before we got there. A lot of them are injured, and our medical crew is on the scene patching up those they can here and loading up others to take to the healers.

Rylee walks out of a nearby building. "I have all the women and children together in one place," she says. "The healers are already there, but I think all this is a lot of emotional shock for these people."

I nod. "We'll get all of them some help, and I'll be sure to get the ones who are vendors compensated for the goods they lost."

Rylee looks around, rubbing her hands together. "Well, we'd better get to work cleaning all this up." Without another word, she walks off and starts picking up the broken tables and tents.

I shrug, smile, and join her.

Braden

I'm about to go out of my mind. It's been two days, and we haven't found Daphne, or whatever her name is. I can't believe I don't even know the name of my mate. I have to find her before I lose what's left of my sanity.

Since my pack is closest to Northside, I've been able to mind-link with some of my pack mates and got a message to Daniel, my Beta, to bring every warrior we've got. He's sent messengers along to Alessandro's and Damon's packs giving their Betas the same orders.

Now, people are pouring into Northside, something none of our packs have ever done before. We're in the closest thing to a city here, which is more of a small town where a few people have been trying to get by on very few supplies for what must have been a long time judging by how run-down the place is. It's not easy to talk to any of these people since most of them are here because they ran away from one of our packs for one reason or another, usually because they've done something illegal, though a few of them just seem to be ordinary people who like being away from it all, I guess.

But finally, Alessandro has gotten a group of people to open up about a village over to the east of this place.

"It's a witch living there, that's f'sure," one woman says. "Does some weird stuff up there. Have some kinda special herbs or something. I don't know. I'm sure not plannin' on goin' there myself."

The mention of the witch has me intrigued. The way Daphne had disappeared so quickly without a trace of her scent had to mean that some magic was behind it. "Could you give us directions to it, please?
"

"Oh, you don't wanna go there," she said.

"We don't, but we have to," Damon said. "We need you to give us directions. You'll be rewarded for your cooperation."

"Can't think o'anything I would want." She looks around at the others, who obviously need quite a lot. "Well, I s'pose we could use some shipments of food here and there."

"Done," Damon said. "Now, please tell us where to find this village."

It takes some time, far longer than I have patience for, for the woman and her friends to give us coherent directions for how to get to this village with the witch. It seems like the best lead we have—the only lead—so we alert our Betas and take off in one of the new cars they've brought.

That gets us most of the way there, but as the women have warned us, all semblance of a road tapers off long before we reach the village, and we have to abandon the car and trudge into the forest.

We arrange our backpacks with clothes in a way that our wolves can easily carry them then shift, flying through the forest as quickly as we can. My paws barely touch the forest floor, I'm running so fast. I don't have any proof, but something in my soul tells me I'm close to her.

Finally, we reach what must be the village, but it's truly the most dilapidated group of houses I've ever seen in my life. Most don't even have roofs anymore, just moss-covered sticks with huge gaps, many sunken down so low that the occupants must have to duck to walk around the dwelling.

We shift back and get dressed on the edge of the forest, though we know we've already been spotted. People who were standing around outside the buildings scurry like mice inside, not that the houses provide much protection from intruders. As we approach, Damon is the first to speak.

"Whoever is in charge here, get out here and talk to us now." He uses his Alpha voice, which is particularly strong since he's next in line for the Alpha King throne.

It works, apparently, because an old, skinny man in tattered clothes comes out of the closest building. "I am Gabriel. I am in charge here. And you speak with the voice of the Alpha King."

"I do," Damon says. "I'm Alpha King Heir Damon Barlowe."

Gabriel gives the sign of respect, at least as well as he can manage to do so in his frail state. Frankly, I'm surprised he can stand. "How can our modest village help the heir to the throne?"

"We're looking for a woman who was kidnapped," I say, not bothering to introduce myself but in too much of a hurry to care. "She has long, curly black hair and blue eyes. Have you seen her?"

Gabriel neither confirms nor denies seeing Daphne, though a few of the people who are brave enough to walk up to us react as though they know who I'm talking about.

"So, you know her," I say. "Where is she?"

"That is the sorceress Coraline to tell, not us," a small older woman says.

Damon looks at the woman. "Coraline?"

"Do you know who that is?" I ask.

He doesn't answer me but instead asks the woman, "What does she look like?"

"Violet hair, grey eyes," she says.

I still don't know what's going on, but Damon's eyes go wide. He starts to say something but then stops when another woman walks by with a basket full of herbs. He runs up to her and sniffs it. "What is this?" he demands.

The woman looks frightened, but the first woman walks over. "That's birdswood. It grows in this forest, and we collect it for the sorceress. In return, she brings food for the village."

"What does it do?"

I don't know why he's asking that when we need to hurry up and find Daphne.

Gabriel steps toward Damon. "It's very powerful. When consumed, it makes the person very easy to control, and they start to lose their wits. After a while, all they want is the herb, and they only speak gibberish."

Damon looks like he's ready to rip off someone's head, and the villagers wisely take a step back.

"Damon, what's going on?" Alessandro asks before I get a chance to say anything.

"This so-called sorceress has been seeing my father, saying she's a healer, for decades," he growls. "All this time she's been poisoning him. No wonder he acts that way." He looks at Gabriel. "Is there an antidote?"

"Yes, there's another herb called rosewind, and we collect that too, though the sorceress never wants much of that."

"We need all you have," I say.

Finally, everything makes sense. Damon's father never used to be as crazy as he is now. I remember him taking time to play catch with us when we were kids, and he seemed level-headed and kind back then.

This is valuable information, but we still haven't found Daphne, and I'm afraid we're running out of time.

Suddenly, Alessandro, Damon, and I all freeze. I can tell by their faces that they're both hearing the same voice in their heads as I am.

'Guys, are you there?'

21

RESCUE

Trisha

'*Damon? Thank the Goddess.*'

He's the first one to answer me, but then the other two chime in shortly after. It's the first time I've been able to mind-link with anyone in this kingdom, and I suppose that's because I'm their mate, though we haven't had any time to make it official.

Thankfully, the little boy had found the key, and stepping out of the cell had opened up the mind-link. There must have been something on the cell walls preventing it.

They're still calling me Daphne, but now isn't the time to explain who I really am. I need to get out of here first and explain later in person.

'*Where are you?*' Braden asks.

'*It's underground, apparently,*' I say. '*A dungeon. I don't see any windows.*'

'*It's okay,*' Damon says. '*I think we're close. We're in a village, and it seems like we can feel you close. Are you alone?*'

'*Yes.*' I nod even though no one can see me. '*They were having the little boy bring me food. He got the key for me. Maybe he's from that village —little boy, brown hair, thin with tattered clothes.'*

'That describes nearly everyone here,' Alessandro says.

'*I promised him I'd help out his village,'* I say, wandering around trying to find a door.

'We'll take care of that,' Damon says. 'We have half our warriors here and logistics forces from our packs. Don't worry about anything. Just find a way out so we can get you.'

'*I think I see a door.'* Up ahead I see what looks like a blue steel door, but the handle doesn't budge. I describe it to my Alphas and hope they see the same thing from the outside.

My Alphas—it's the first time I've called them that, even though it's only in my mind. I never thought I wanted a single mate, but now, I can't imagine a life without all three of them. I just need to get out of here first so we can be together.

"All right, little lady."

I startle at the deep voice and whirl around. The man is tall, but he's thin and doesn't look very strong. Still, I don't know what kind of potion they gave me or magic they did to knock me out before, so I know I'm not exactly in peak shape.

"Now, are you gonna make this easy, or are we gonna do it the fun way?" He gave a suggestive smirk that makes bile rise in my throat.

'Guys, I could really use some help right now,' I say in the mind-link.

'We're coming,' Alessandro says. 'There's a villager here who knows about an old mine shaft that we think could be your dungeon. It's not far.'

'Please hurry,' I say, though I know they're doing the best they can.

I take a deep breath and look around. Since I turned on the lights when I left the cell, I see that there are some metal shovels nearby I could use as weapons, and I try to figure out how I can trick him into lunging at me in one direction so I can sneak by the other side and grab it.

But then, I remember—I'm twenty-one, and I can shift. I've never done it before, and I don't know if it'll hurt, or if I'll be too slow at it, or if this guy who's after me will have a bigger wolf than me, but I decide pretty quickly that I'm going to do it anyway.

'How close are you?' I ask my Alphas.

'We found it! We're working on the door,' Braden tells me.

The guy in front of me suddenly gets a whole new level of creepy in his expression and moves toward me, and I decide I need to do something now. I can't wait for the Alphas to get through the lock.

'You might want to back up the black wolf,' I say, guessing what I'll probably look like in wolf form before I focus all my attention on shifting. It comes faster and easier than I'd imagined it, completely painless and even liberating. I feel more energy radiating through my veins than I've ever felt.

And there's one more thing I wasn't expecting—I'm huge. Well, I'm not a giant wolfzilla or anything. That would be silly. But I'm a good enough sized wolf to make the creepy guy's eyes just about bulge out of his head. He doesn't seem so tall anymore even though he's still taller than me, but I have no fear in my heart when I lunge at him.

He turns and runs, shifting midway into a scrawny looking grey wolf. I've just started running after him when the door behind me bursts open, and a huge white wolf—bigger than me—runs past me and makes a flying leap toward the grey wolf. He takes him down in no time and turns around. I see the silver eyes and know instantly it's Alessandro.

In this form, the mate bond feels even stronger, and the way he's looking at me tells me he's processing it fully himself. I know the Alphas knew I was their mate long before I did, but there's something about having that final proof that's very intense.

The scent of apples and strawberries multiplies exponentially, and I discover that Damon and Braden's wolves are right beside me. I have the same moment with them, and we all feel like we're frozen in time for a moment while we feel the intensity of the bond.

Braden breaks the silence in the mind-link. *'Is there anyone else down here that we need to take care of?'*

I shake my head, too stunned to even speak in my mind. I'm sure the woman and the man who spoke before are long gone.

He chuckles, which is always a strange thing to experience in a mind-link. *'Do you know that even your wolf has curly hair?'*

I look down at my paw and notice a little curl on my legs, and I turn around to look at what I can see of my body. He's right. It's nowhere near as curly as my human hair, but it definitely has a wave to it. It's deep black and kind of pretty, actually.

'Your clothes are history, but we have some upstairs,' Damon says. *'Let's just get out of here and we'll worry about the mate stuff later.'*

I nod, and we head out the door and up the stairs where I find myself in the middle of the forest. A female warrior, who apparently belongs to one of the Alpha's packs, runs up to me and takes some clothes out of a backpack and guides me behind a tree where I easily shift back for the first time and get dressed.

It's a bit of an adjustment going from a strong, big wolf to a human female, even though I am in good shape. It takes me a minute to get a hold of my center of gravity again, then the woman leads me back to my Alphas.

I wrap my arms around Alessandro first since he's closest to me. I don't want to let go, but I'm drawn to the other two as well, so I take turns holding all of them. I have a strong urge to kiss them all—and probably do a lot more than that with them—but we're standing in the middle of the forest with several support warriors standing by staring at us.

Yeah, not exactly a private moment.

"I'm so glad you're safe," Braden says. "Did they hurt you?"

I shrug. "Not really, though they knocked me out or drugged me with something at first. I don't know what that was."

"It's probably these damn plants," Damon says with a low growl. "Which reminds me. We need to get the hell out of here and back to my father before he actually starts fighting the Dark Forest kingdom."

"What?" I ask.

"Come on," Alessandro says. "We'll explain on the way."

We start heading out and come across a clearing with several buildings that are so dilapidated they can barely be called houses, and I see a familiar face.

"Aryx!" I holler. He turns around and sees me but looks terribly frightened of all the Alphas surrounding me. "Give me a second, okay, guys?" I ask.

They nod and stay back while I walk up to the boy slowly. I kneel to be closer to his height. "You did such a wonderful job saving me," I say. "We're going to take care of you and your village, and we'll do what we can to find your parents, okay? I promise, you won't have to worry about eating or having a safe place to sleep ever again."

He nods, and I give him a very gentle hug. When I pull back, he's actually smiling. A female warrior walks up.

"I can take it from here," she says. "I promise, he'll be fine."

"Did you hear that?" I say to the boy. "This lady will help you. I have to leave now, but I'll be back, I promise."

Aryx nods, and I give him another quick hug before leaving him with the woman.

"She's a healer from my pack," Damon explains. "We've instructed everyone here to relocate these people to somewhere safe and comfortable and give them everything they need."

"Thank you," I say.

We all get into an SUV where my bag, the one I'd originally brought to Green Mountain, is sitting on the seat. It sparks a memory, and I pick it up, digging through it to find the one item I'd brought with me that had seemed frivolous at the time.

"There was a woman there in the dungeon," I explain to my Alphas. "She sounded so evil. For some reason, she and a man she was talking to mentioned my wolf statue here." I pull it out to show them. "Do you have any idea why?"

They all shake their heads. "No idea," Alessandro says. "But I'm sure once we get back to Damon's castle, they'll be some scholars that could take a look at it and let you know if they recognize it."

With Damon in the driver's seat, we head out of Northside while the Alphas explain to me what had happened to his father. Apparently, a witch disguised as a healer has been drugging him with some sort of tea for decades, one that she got from Aryx's rundown village, and it left him under her full control.

And he's about to attack Dark Forest.

"Guys, I guess it's time to tell you something," I say.

Alessandro and Braden turn to look at me, and Damon glances up into the rearview mirror.

"My real name is Trisha Forrest-Stone, princess of Dark Forest."

22

A NEW LUNA QUEEN

Braden

WE'RE ALL SHOCKED, even Damon, who's not easily surprised. He pulls over the car and practically slams on the brakes so we all lurch forward. He turns the car off, faces Daphne—Trisha—and starts to speak before I've even processed it all.

"You're a princess from Dark Forest?" he asks, his tone higher than usual.

"Sorry, I guess I shouldn't have said that while you were driving," she says.

"But it's true?" Alessandro chimes in.

"Yes," she says. "I'm one of the Luna Queen's four children. Tristan Stone is my father."

Damon takes a breath. "So it's likely those people knew who you were and targeted you, the ones who kidnapped you."

"It's likely," she says with a nod.

"All right." Damon restarts the car. "We need to get to my father."

We don't say a lot for the rest of the ride, which is long. About halfway through, we switch drivers so Damon can get some rest, though frankly he seems wired up enough to make it the whole way. I think we all want to talk, but we all feel the tension. Damon's father is about to attack our mate's homeland, and all we can think about it is stopping it.

As we finally reach Westmont and approached the castle, we all open up a bit. I guess we've had time to absorb the news.

"What's it like in Dark Forest?" I ask. I've always heard it is an awful place, but it can't be if Trisha is from there.

"Honestly, it's about the same as here," she says. "I don't know why we don't trade regularly or share technology."

"That figures," Damon says. "You have no idea how bad they've brainwashed us to think that Dark Forest is full of thieves and murderers."

Trisha chuckles. "It sounds like we had the same education. Teachers in school tell the kids it's horrible here, and they don't even know anything about it."

"I was pretty surprised when I went there," Alessandro says.

She turns to look at him. "Why were you there?"

He nods toward Damon. "The Alpha King Heir here sent me to see if what his father was rattling on about was true. Of course it wasn't." We're quiet for a few moments until Alessandro adds, "So how do you think those people knew you? That ship we were on is the only one that comes here, and that's rare, maybe once a month at most. It's amazing that you chose it."

"I didn't choose it. Whatever was guiding me here did," she says. "And I really don't know. I guess it could have been anyone who recognized me. What did you say that witch's name was?"

"Coraline," Damon says with a bit of a growl in his voice. I know he's anxious to get to his father now that we know he's being poisoned. I hope we're not too late.

"Hmm." Trisha turns and faces ahead, watching the road, but she doesn't say more.

We arrive at the castle and practically run inside. I know Damon's mind-linking everyone to find his father, and after running down a couple of hallways, we find him in the library. But he's not reading. He's sitting in a chair… facing a wall.

"Father?" Damon asks.

The king looks up like he's surprised. "Oh, my boy! It's so good to see you."

"It's—um—good to see you too." Damon stares at his father, and the king's Beta comes into the library, still panting after an apparent long run.

"He's been this way for hours," he whispers. "I've had the healer come in, but she doesn't have a clue what's wrong."

Alessandro hands him a pouch of the antidote herb from Northside. "Make a tea with this, quickly. It's an antidote."

The man doesn't even hesitate, just runs out of the room with it.

Damon pulls a chair up next to the king. "Father, I need to talk to you."

The king turns his head again. "Oh, Damon! It's good to see you, my boy! Did you bring me a lollipop?"

"Um…." I look at Alessandro and Trisha, and they both shrug.

"What do you mean, Father?" I've never seen Damon look so worried, and I've known him all my life.

"You went to the candy store for me, right?" the king asks. "Didn't I give you enough change?"

"Just go with it," I whisper. I figure it's probably better to play along. Clearly, there's something wrong with the man's mind.

Damon nods. "Oh, I didn't realize you wanted one too. I'll have to go back there." The Beta walks into the room, and Damon takes the hot cup from him and shows it to his father. "Look, Beta Kurt has your tea."

The king sniffs it. "It doesn't smell like my tea."

"This is a special kind," Damon explains. "Coraline gave this to me to give you."

Beta Kurt steps back beside me and whispers, "I know this is going against the Alpha King's orders, but I'm going to go ahead and go with this and ask for forgiveness later."

"I think his son is in charge at this point anyway," I whisper back. "Clearly, the Alpha King is incapacitated. No one will blame you."

He nods, and we continue to watch as Damon coaxes the king into drinking a few sips of the antidote. I don't expect it will work right away. It seems like this is long-term damage that might not even be reversible.

"I'm very tired," the king says. "I think I'd like to sleep now."

"I'll help you to your quarters, Your Majesty," Kurt says. As he escorts the king away, he whispers, "I'll ensure that the healer watches over him. And we'll give him more of this."

"Thank you, Beta Kurt," Damon says.

I wait a moment because I know he's mind-linking everyone in the kingdom who can stop the war. He's the acting Alpha King now, so we have a chance to stop this.

"It's no use," he finally says. "The fighting has already begun."

Ethan

After a long day of cleanup, we're exhausted. Everything in the marketplace has been taken care of, and our people are working on getting everyone compensated for the goods they lost. Unfortunately, there have been some deaths from the rogue attacks. All we can do is be sure their families are supported.

We're ready to get out of here now, and Matthew gets into the car in front of us we collapse into our SUV, and Rylee leans against me. I reach my arm around her to settle her in more comfortably.

"I'm so impressed with you," I say.

She chuckles and lifts her head. "Oh? I think that giant red wolf of yours did some damage as well."

I laugh, wrapping my fingers around hers. "It was incredible, shifting like that. I didn't think it would be so easy."

"As I told you, you're a child of the moon," she says. "Everything about you is unique. The kingdom will be proud of you... except that your mate is a friend of rogues."

She chuckles at this, but I cradle her chin in my hand, gently lifting her head to eye level. "My mate is beautiful, caring, and loving. She's a friend to everyone in the kingdom, and she will be respected as such. It's a beautiful thing you did today, helping all those people get to safety. You're going to make an incredible Luna." I move in closer, bringing her mouth to mine and enjoying her taste on my lips and then my tongue as we deepen the kiss.

She moves closer, wrapping her arms around me and propping one leg up on mine to turn herself more toward me. Her jet-black hair falls around my shoulders, and I run my fingers through it. It's so soft, like silk, and my cock stiffens with the close proximity of her inner thigh.

But I realize that we have no privacy here, and the driver and front seat occupant squirm uncomfortably in their seats.

"We'd better save this for back in the castle," I whisper.

She giggles and nods. "I'll try to control myself, but it's not easy."

"I hear that."

We both laugh and separate, and I swear I can hear a sigh of relief from the front seat. I know they would have kept their cool even if we'd gone full-on hot and heavy, but that wouldn't have been fair to them.

I pass Rylee a water bottle from the cooler and grab one for myself, and the ice-cold water helps... a little. I can't wait to get home and really show her how I'm feeling.

But for now, we cool off.

"I recognized some of those wolves," she says suddenly.

I look at her. "Was Calvin one of them?"

She shakes her head. "No, but some of his officers were in the attack. Calvin is a coward. He doesn't even fight anymore, just has others do his dirty work. I don't know whether you've captured any of the officers since I was with the women and children most of the time. I'd like to look at them to identify them if I can have the chance."

"Of course," I say. "They're all going straight to the dungeon."

"Will they be executed?" she asks.

I take a breath. "Of course not. Why would you—oh, I guess that's what they've all been saying about my mother and fathers."

"I'm sorry," she says. "That's how the rogues would handle anyone they captured. I guess I'm just too used to being on the wrong side of things."

"There shouldn't be a side," I say. "Everyone in this kingdom is a citizen, whether they're recognized in a pack or not. We've come a long way since King Gene and the evil people who guided his rule. I know we still have more work to do. My brother and I will finish the job, I promise."

She nods. "So you'll rule equally together?"

"That's the plan," I say. "The kingdom will have two Alpha Kings and two Luna Queens." I touch her cheek. "You'll be one of them."

"I guess I haven't thought much about that," she says.

I nod. "I think you'll do a great job helping the rogues feel like they belong."

"Maybe we'll start by not calling them rogues anymore."

I nod again. "Good point. See? You're doing better than me already."

She laughs. "I'm doing well with you because we're partners."

"That we are."

I'm about to kiss her again when my father Eli's voice comes in through the mind-link.

'Oh, thank the Goddess you're in range,' he says.

'What's wrong?' I ask.

'There's a skirmish at the port. The kingdom is under attack.'

2 3

THE EVE OF BATTLE

Trisha

I CAN FEEL Damon's pain. It must have been so hard for him to watch his father slowly deteriorate into this state when he didn't understand what was happening. I don't know anything about his past yet. We haven't even had time to talk, but I look in his eyes and see the ache in his soul.

We still don't have time to talk. My kingdom is already under attack. Even with Damon temporarily in charge, there's nothing he can do.

We stand around for a few moments letting the news sink in. I want to go home and warn everyone, and I want to do something to stop people from fighting. They have to know that they've been led by a man who was poisoned into madness. But I remember how long it took to get here by ship, and I know that even if I leave today, I won't get there for weeks, and by then, it will be too late.

But apparently, my Alphas have been doing more than just absorbing the shocking news.

"The pilot will meet us there," Alessandro says.

"We don't have time to pack anything," Braden chimes in. "I don't know what we're going to need."

"There are stores in Dark Forest," Damon says. He looks at me. "Right?"

"What? Yes, stores...."

Recognition flashes in my mind. They'd said pilot.

They had a plane.

"The Council is waiting for us in the main hall," Damon adds.

"The who?" But no one answers me as they all start moving, and Damon takes my hand.

"We'll explain on the way," he says.

He starts to pull me because my legs don't quite move right away, but seconds later, I'm running with my Alphas down the castle hallways. We reach a giant room where a couple of older men are standing. We walk up to them, not saying anything.

I realize that they're just leaving me out of the conversation. *'Want to let me in on it?'* I ask Damon in the mind-link, and seconds later it's like a floodgate opens because I hear the entire conversation between these men, my Alphas, and some other people who are apparently running to get to the room as quickly as they can.

This is their kingdom's High Council, and this is Damon's coronation ceremony.

The healer and the Beta speak in the open mind-link, the former verifying that the current Alpha King is mentally incapacitated and the latter agreeing that Alpha King Roland can no longer perform his duties.

A woman runs into the room, followed by a man, and they take their place next to the older men we'd been waiting with. Other people follow who look like servants, and one is carrying a large gold box.

"We're ready to begin," one of the men says. He looks like the oldest. He turns and looks at Damon. "Prince Damon Barlowe, it has come to the attention of this Council that your father, Alpha King Roland Barlowe, is unable to perform his duties as Alpha King of Green Mountain. In accordance with our laws, with agreement from the entire Council, the Alpha King's Beta, and the royal healer, we may pass the torch to you. All in favor?"

One by one, the Council members say, "Aye."

The healer and Beta Kurt say the same in the open mind-link.

"By the power afforded us by the laws of Green Mountain and with guidance from the Goddess, we pronounce you Alpha King Damon Barlowe."

The man with the box steps forward, and the Council member pulls out a crown, which he places on Damon's head followed by an emerald-green sash that goes from his shoulders to his hip, and a pin that he attaches to his collar.

Damon bows his head and says, "Accepted." He takes off the crown and sash and puts them back in the box just seconds later, keeping the pin.

"Now, please go stop this crazy war," the old man says.

Damon nods and takes my hand again, and we all rush out of the castle and into a large SUV.

"Wow," Alessandro says as we settle in and the driver takes off. "Are you all right, man?"

"Yeah," Damon says. "I know he'll be okay. He's been drinking that tea for a long time. It's going to take a while for all that to undo itself. I trust Kurt. They've been friends for years."

"I'm sure he'll be fine," I say. I don't know that for sure, but I have a feeling the antidote will work.

He takes my hand and squeezes it. I feel a pleasant spark of electricity run up my arm, and I realize that I haven't had any time at all to be physical with my mates.

I've heard all the stories about it. People see their mates for the first time across a crowded room, and all they want to do is touch each other. They kiss, and they can't pull away. They end up with the man sweeping the woman off her feet and carrying her off where they can be alone, making mad, passionate love for days on end without coming up for air.

All I've had is a hug and hand holding, and I have three mates.

We have a lot to make up for.

But I feel a little guilty because my other two mates are sitting across from me, facing us, and I can't give them the same physical contact.

Alessandro seems to read my mind because he's suddenly in it–in a private mind-link. *'It's okay,'* he says. *'We'll all have a chance to be with you. Right now, Damon is the one who needs the most support.'*

I smile at Alessandro and he smiles back. I squeeze Damon's hand and feel his body relaxing.

We reach the airport quickly and drive right up to the plane on the runway. It doesn't look like this place is used often, but I suppose since no one wants to fly to Dark Forest or other kingdoms, there isn't much call for one this big. I notice several small planes around that look like they've been used more for local trips.

We're already in our seats, which are more like sofas in the huge private plane, when a sudden mind-link opens. Damon is talking to the pilot, and since they're mid-conversation, he apparently just remembered to include me. The man sounds excited, and he says we're ready to go.

It's a smooth takeoff, and soon we're up at altitude.

"This will take all night," Damon says. "There's a bed in the back. You should go get some sleep, Trisha."

"Go with her," Braden says. "You need the rest just as much as she does."

"I agree," Alessandro says. He looks at me. "We'll each have plenty of time with you. Tonight, it'll be Damon's turn, okay?"

I nod, thankful that I'm finally going to have some time to relax with one of them at least. We stand and hold hands as he leads me back to the private bedroom in the rear of the plane.

I've never been with a man. I've never even kissed one, unless you count the boy back in third grade that I kissed on the cheek on a dare.

Damon seems to sense that I'm not experienced in this sort of thing as he moves exceedingly gently and takes his time.

He starts by kissing me gently as we sit on the bed beside each other. His scent, which was making me angry only a few days ago, is now so irresistible I can taste it on him. I learn quickly why people enjoy kissing so much, and I get an even better thrill when he introduces his tongue. I part my lips for him, and it feels so natural to just let my tongue dance with his.

In a few minutes, he leans me back, lifting me slightly, effortlessly, so I'm more in the middle of the bed, and my head is on the pillow.

We get back to kissing, and I can't get enough of it. I wrap my arms around him and pull him closer, and now I feel his right hand running up and down my side, settling on my hip. The feeling of his hands so close to my core gives me a warm sensation that rushes up my spine.

I can feel the thrill of my wolf as he touches me–my mate. No one has ever mentioned it before, but having my wolf feels like there is a distinct personality inside me, my most base, animalistic desires, and right now, she's awakened in the presence of her mate.

I moan as his hands reach to unzip my jeans and I help him along, slipping out of them and my panties at once. I don't want to waste a single second. Hearing his low moan, I know Damon approves.

His fingers migrate to my pussy at once, stroking it with light, circular motions as he plays in my juices. I spread my legs wide as he explores me. Every stroke of his fingers causes pleasant shivers and makes me even wetter.

He reaches up with his other hand under my shirt, and I quickly pull it up over my head. I don't bother with the bra because he has unclasped it already and pushed it up for access to my nipples, which he plays with while his other hand continues to stroke me down below.

He stops after a moment and moves on top of me, giving me a gentle kiss and stroking my hair. He takes his clothes off but stops to look into my eyes before he goes farther.

"I'll be gentle."

I nod as I spread my legs even farther apart, and I feel him pushing inside me. I expect it to hurt and prepare myself, but it doesn't. He's huge, and I have no idea how he's fitting inside me, but once he pushes past a certain spot, it feels like heaven, like I'm finally complete. It's the most intense physical and emotional experience I've ever had.

It's so clear that we're made for each other. After I get used to it, I match his stroke, pushing out against him as he's pushing in.

"Harder," I say, and he obliges, picking up our rhythm, stroking me harder and faster.

Something changes. A new, intense feeling emerges, and I start to cry out. It feels like going over the edge, and I feel him stiffen even more just before we both explode, and a warm sensation washes over me.

We continue to cling to each other, our hearts pounding in sync and slowing together as our breathing gradually returns to normal.

I must have passed out because I wake up in what seems like just a few moments to kisses from a fully dressed Damon.

"We land in ten minutes, beautiful," he says.

ETHAN

WE DON'T EVEN head to the castle. We just reroute the entire convoy of warriors, minus the ambulances and prisoner transports, toward the port.

From what my father has told us, soldiers are pouring in from a fleet of ships flying the Green Mountain colors. No one has heard from anyone in Green Mountain for generations, but apparently, now they have a whole army attacking out of nowhere.

All my dads are scrambling with their allies to meet us there and fight. We all check in through the mind-link.

Matthew reports our position to our dads from the car in front of us. *Ethan and I are five minutes out.*

We're twenty minutes out, my father Eli says. *But I have a big team ready.*

My other dads report in after him.

'My troops are heading in from the south,' Tristan says. *'I'm guessing fifteen minutes.'*

'Ten minutes for my team,' Mark chimes in. *'Ethan and Matthew, it looks like you'll be there first. Assess the situation. If it's too much for the warriors you have, especially after you handled the issue at the marketplace, hold back until the rest of us get there.'*

I look at Rylee and wish she wasn't with me. She'd done well holding her own during the marketplace attack, but everything in my being is screaming for her to be as far away from danger as she can be. I know that's a combination of my love for her and the mate bond, which I realize makes me overprotective.

But I know she's a strong woman. I know she wants to help and I need to trust that she will be careful.

That's easier said than done.

Rylee squeezes my hand. "We've got this."

2 4

HOME AGAIN

Trisha

I DON'T HAVE much time to get dressed, but thankfully there's a good-sized restroom in this area of the plane where I quickly get ready and make myself presentable. It occurs to me that we didn't use any kind of birth control last night, but I just shrug it off. If the Moon Goddess has given me three Alpha mates, then I'm sure She'll make children happen when it's the right time as well.

Being with Damon was amazing, and I can't wait to have time with my other two mates. I'm sure they're anxious to get to that part themselves, though they were very understanding about waiting while Damon and I had our time together. I suppose that's why I'm mates with those three.

It's sort of like my dads. My parents never elaborated on the sexual part of their relationship to us kids, of course, but as I got older, I figured out that they took turns spending the night with Mom. It seems to have worked for them. I guess I'll need to talk to my Alphas about a similar arrangement.

I step out of the restroom, and Damon smiles at me. "You look beautiful." He kisses me, and I close my eyes as we linger a few moments, just enjoying the taste of each other. He breaks the moment and touches my cheek with his palm. "I don't want to leave this bedroom, but we'd better get in our seats for landing."

I nod and take his hand, going back up to the main cabin to see Alessandro and Braden in their same seats.

"Hey, sleepyhead," Braden says. "I was wondering whether we'd need to come get you for the landing."

"Hey," I say. "Good morning. I hope you guys weren't too uncomfortable."

"Not at all," Alessandro says. "These little couches fold out into beds. This is some plane, Damon. I could get used to this."

We laugh for a second, but then it's clear that Damon has opened another mind-link and we all listen in.

'There's no way to land,' the pilot says. *'It looks like some fighting at the port has spilled into the runway area.'*

I should have thought of that. It makes sense that Roland's people are attacking at the port since they came by ship, and the main airport is right by there. *'Fly north,'* I say. *'There's a smaller airport near the coast about thirty miles north of this one.'*

'Aye, aye.'

'Do we have enough fuel?' Alessandro asks.

'Yes, that's not a problem.'

The mind-link closes, and I sit next to Damon on one of the sofas, across from my other Alphas. "That one's a better choice anyway," I explain. "It's closer to the castle. I'll see if I can reach my sister and have her send a car."

As soon as we are close enough, I contacted Reeva.

'Trisha! Oh, my Goddess, you're alive! We thought you were gone forever! Why didn't you contact me before? I've been so worried about you.'

I want to answer all her questions, but we don't have time for that. *'I'll tell you everything later. Please send a car to Beach Pack Airport. I'll come to the castle. We're landing soon.'*

'You're flying? We? Who's with you?'

I laugh. *'You'll see. Send an SUV.'*

'Oh, he'd better be cute.'

I say goodbye so she can get the car ready and giggle a little. It's nice to hear from my sister again. I really miss her, even with my three Alphas following me all over Green Mountain. She's going to have a fit when she learns I went there.

"Everything good?" Braden asks.

I nod. "She just said you guys had better be cute." I laugh again.

"Well, there's no problem there," Alessandro says.

Damon just shakes his head.

The pilot contacts us again and says we're landing, so we get our seatbelts on and wait until we touch the ground again. I don't mind flying. I've done it a few times in little planes that go back and forth between different packs in Dark Forest. But it's always a comfort to land. I guess it's just not natural for wolves to fly.

The car is already waiting when we taxi in. Beach pack is my dad Eli's home pack, Ethan's biological father. Their territory covers most of the southern part of Dark Forest where all the beach resorts are, and Reeva must have asked a friend there to meet us.

The driver is nice, and I ask him to take us to the castle, which is about a thirty-minute drive from here. It feels weird to be so close to home again. I pick up my bag, the same one I snuck out of the castle with, and feel the wolf statue inside. I pull it out.

"I forgot to have someone look this over at your castle," I say to Damon. "I really want to know what they wanted with it."

"We'll give it to one of the scholars when we get back home," he says.

Home—it hadn't occurred to me that this wouldn't be my home anymore. I will be Luna Queen in Green Mountain, a place I'd been afraid of since I was old enough to understand the scary stories about it. I'm not sure how I feel about that.

Again, my Alphas seem to sense my fear.

"It's okay," Alessandro says. "Since you're our mate, we'll connect

Green Mountain with Dark Forest forever. That will mean this won't be the only plane flying between the two kingdoms, and you can visit here whenever you want."

"I guess so," I say. "I've just never even considered that I'd live somewhere else. I mean, I always liked to go out exploring, but this has always been my home base."

"It always will be, in a way," Braden says. "Alessandro is right. It's not going to feel so far away anymore." He pulls me in close since I'm sitting next to him.

It feels good, and his scent is so comforting. It's funny how it's almost the same as Damon's, yet different. It's like it's a different type of apple, very subtle. I guess each one of my mates has a different personality, and their scents match. Braden's is lighter, more relaxed than Damon's. I snuggle in and close my eyes as he strokes my hair.

But that's interrupted soon by a panicked voice in the mind-link.

'Trisha! My baby! Where have you been? Do you have any idea how much I was worried sick about you?'

'Mom, I'm fine. It's okay.'

'It is not okay, young lady. You just wait until your fathers and I—'

'Mom.'

'Trisha?'

'I'm not a kid anymore. I'm a grown woman, and I have mates, three of them, all Alphas.'

'Three!'

'Yes, Mom, three. And I'd love to chat more in our heads, but I'm about to drive through the castle gates.'

'My baby is home!'

I shake my head and put my hand to my forehead. I'll never be anything but a baby to her. And I feel the heat rising in my cheeks as she comes running up to the car shouting the same thing.

I get out as quickly as I can to quiet her down, and she squeezes me so tight I can't say a word yet. Thankfully, my Alphas hold back a bit so I'm not completely embarrassed by the spectacle.

"Mom, I need to breathe," I say finally.

"Oh." She lets me go and smiles at my Alphas. "These must be your mates. My, how handsome you all are."

Damon greets her first. "It's a pleasure to meet you, Luna Queen Rose. I'm Alpha King Damon Barlowe of Green Mountain."

Mom gasps. "Green Mountain! Trisha, I—"

"Mom, they're her mates." Reeva cuts her off, coming up behind us.

I practically squeeze the air out of my sister while Braden and Alessandro meet my mother.

"It's a pleasure, Luna Queen Rose. I'm Braden Winten, Alpha Heir of Western Pine pack. I'm afraid that's in Green Mountain as well."

"And I'm Alessandro Bianchi, Alpha Heir of Chestnut pack, also Green Mountain."

"It's wonderful to meet you all," Mom says. "I'm terribly sorry for my rudeness. I'm just overexcited at having my Trisha back home. This is my other daughter, Reeva."

My Alphas greet Reeva and Mom invites us inside.

"Mom, I wish I had time to fill you in on everything, but we need to talk about the war," I say. "It's urgent."

"Let's go to the front parlor," she says, her expression grim.

I nod, knowing we need to talk about this somewhere private.

"Please, Mom, sit," I say when we get there. "I need to explain this as quickly and simply as I can. Damon's father was the Alpha King, but he was poisoned by a witch named Coraline who posed as a healer for years. She gave him a tea that controlled his mind, and frankly, he's lost control."

I look at Damon, sorry that I have to be so blunt about his father, but he nods, urging me on.

"Anyway, we figured it out because I was kidnapped by them and—"

"Kidnapped? Oh, my baby!"

I know this reminds her of the last time I was kidnapped twenty years ago. But we don't have time for that now. "Mom, I'm fine now. Please, I have to explain this so we can get to the front and stop this. Damon has taken over now, but those warriors came by boat, and they don't know it yet, though he's trying to reach them by mind-link."

I look at him and he shakes his head. "So far, I can't get anyone to answer. They may be ignoring me because they don't know I'm the Alpha King yet. They need to see me so I can show them proof."

I nod and turn back to Mom. "He needs to get out there and stop this foolishness before more people get hurt. Where are the dads?"

"Oh, dear. They all went out fighting with the armies. I stayed back, praying that you'd get here."

"We need to go there, now," I say.

Adam, our lead Beta, and his wife Shelby run in. "Come with us," Adam says.

"How do you—"

Damon cut me off. "I opened a mind-link with the Beta when we got here. I guess as Alpha King, I can speak with people from other kingdoms as well. I just sent out feelers for the Beta. And we have to go."

"I'm going with you," Mom says.

Reeva says she's going too, and there's no time to argue, so we all follow Adam out to the courtyard where a line of SUVs is already there for us, engines running and drivers in their seats.

"Ride with your mother and sister," Damon suggests. "We can still talk in the mind-link."

I nod and get in the car with Mom and Reeva. The drivers don't waste any time heading out.

"Way to go, Trisha," Reeva says. "Those guys are gorgeous hunks times three."

We all giggle. Since I finally have a few minutes with Mom and Reeva, I explain how I'd gotten on the ship, got lost in the port city in Green Mountain, found my way to Northside and found the little boy who'd been calling me in my dream, all the while having my Alphas annoying me by saving me from myself all along the way.

"So, you finally got to settle that," Reeva says. "I'm glad. And I can't believe you have three mates. I haven't found mine yet, Matthew either. But Ethan found his out at Raven pack."

"Just one?" I ask.

She laughs. "Just one. Now I'm wondering about mine."

"You'll find him soon."

"Or them," she says.

"Or them." We laugh again, but I can't help worrying about the battle. I hope we reach them in time and that everyone listens to their new Alpha King.

2 5

UNITING THE KINGDOMS

Ethan

I LOOK AT RYLEE, wishing she were safe at the castle but also knowing that there's no way she would stay behind and wait for me. But I realize from the look in her eyes that, once again, she doesn't intend to go directly into battle.

"There are innocents around here," she says. "I'm going to get as many people to safety as I can."

We kiss deeply but quickly, and once again, I watch her run away and take hold of a woman with a small child. The woman is just standing there paralyzed in the middle of the road watching all the fighting around her.

Rylee isn't safe at home where I'd really like her to be, but she knows how to keep herself safe when danger is around. I have to trust her so I can go do what I need to. I turn and face the battle, shifting and giving orders to my warriors as I quickly map out the best strategy.

These guys are tough and organized, obviously well trained. Instead of a band of rogues without formal training, we're facing a kingdom's army. I slip in and take out a couple of them in the front. My heart isn't in it because I have no idea why these people are attacking us all of a sudden, but I have to protect the people of my kingdom.

All my dads and their warriors arrive in army transports at the same time, and each of the armies they're with from the many different packs in the kingdom take up different positions.

'These guys are well-trained,' I warn them in the mind-link.

'Roger that,' Tristan says.

Soon we're in a good position and move in for the strike, but the enemy's reinforcements keep arriving by ship. It's like an endless supply of them, and we already have as many warriors here as we can mobilize quickly. I know the others are getting ready or traveling farther, but for now, we have to fight with what we have.

I take out as many enemy warriors as I can, still feeling guilty because I don't know why these people are fighting us. But they've killed some of our warriors now, so there's no stopping the carnage that's about to happen.

My dads and I are thick in the fray, our larger wolves overpowering several of their smaller ones, even though there are constantly more enemies arriving in small boats from the large fleet of ships offshore. It stretches as far as I can see in every direction. There must be fifty thousand warriors here, and for some reason, they're bent on destroying us.

I catch a glimpse of a woman in human form and do a double-take because she's on one of the small boats arriving with enemies. It throws me off for a second as I see her get off on the dock and run away, her purple hair trailing behind her.

Whoever she is, I'll have to deal with her later because I have my hands full with the wolves in front of me. I still don't see any the size of me, Matthew, or my dads. There don't seem to be any royals participating in this battle at all, which is strange. We've always had an Alpha lead the charge. Maybe things are different in Green Mountain.

A scraggly gray wolf almost overpowers me while I'm distracted, but I snap out of it fast and take care of him quickly. There are going to be so many dead wolves on the docks when we're through here. I don't even want to imagine what that will be like.

I take out a few more and leap onto a shipping container to get a better view of the battle. It's a hell of a place for a war. Normally, we'd be in the field away from civilians. Wars were between the wolves who had a problem, and the winners would govern those who happened to be in that territory.

But this was a full-on assault on a civilian target. Besides the shipping lanes, there's a wharf out here that attracts tourists with its seafood restaurants and mini museums. Sometimes kids even come here on school field trips. Goddess, I hope there aren't any children here today.

'Please see if there are any kids on the wharf,' I mind-link to Rylee.

'Already cleared,' she answers. *'Be safe out there. This looks bad.'*

'I will,' I say. *'Rylee, I love you.'*

'I love you, too, Ethan.'

I have to close the mind-link because a group of angry warriors is coming my way. Two of my warriors back me up, and I jump off the container and into the fray.

There's a group of about a dozen and only three of us. Most of them are smaller, and my warriors make quick work of them with bites to their necks. I shift quickly, running up to the largest wolf, which looks to be a Beta.

I don't want to fight him. I don't want to fight any of them, but they brought this to our shores. I leap forward, twisting my head in a maneuver designed to grab him by the neck, but he dodges my attack and rolls away, quickly getting up and running toward me.

I use a technique Tristan taught me, ducking and spinning around in such a way that I end up under the enemy wolf with my teeth right under his neck. I take him out with a single bite and jump up to face the rest of them.

A couple of them run off and the warriors and I handle the ones who remain easily.

Happy for the victory, I look up. The boats keep coming. I'm not sure how much longer we can hold these troops back.

Damon

I sit in the car with Alessandro and Braden, wishing I was holding hands with my mate. I guess I need to think of her as our mate since she's also mated to my two best friends. It's not something any of us ever thought about, and having these few moments in the car gives us another chance to discuss it.

"Am I supposed to call 'dibs' if I'm next?" Braden laughs, but I don't think it's funny. Alessandro scolds him before I get the chance.

"She's our mate, buddy," he says. "Have some respect."

"I have a huge amount of respect for Trisha," he insists. "I just don't know how we're supposed to do this. Do we take turns every night? Or do we have like a week that's our turn?"

"This is a conversation we need to have with Trisha," I say. "Yes, we'll have to take turns somehow, but I think she should be the one to decide how that goes. She might need some time because last night was her first time with a man."

"I can't say I don't wish it had been with me," Alessandro says.

"Me too," Braden admits.

"It's going to be different with all of us," I say. "Her first time with you is going to be special because you're her mate, both of you."

"Should we ask her now?" Alessandro asks.

I shake my head. "Let her have some time with her mother and sister instead of talking sex with her in her head." I laugh at that, and the other two join me. "Her mother seems like a kind lady, and she should talk to her now when she has a chance. Trisha will probably be returning to Green Mountain with us, or I hope she will. We should give her some time with her family without distractions."

Alessandro's eyes go a little wide. "I never even considered that she might not return with us. Do you think there's a chance of that?"

"I don't think so," Braden says. "But I agree that she does need to be with her family for a while."

We stop talking because we start to see people running, and we know we're getting closer to the battleground. There's a huge traffic jam on the other side of the street heading in the opposite direction as people try to escape, but this side of the street is empty. No one's stupid enough to head toward a war, except us, I suppose.

As we approach, I'm frantically trying to communicate with the commanders in my mind-link. But they're either telling me they're under Alpha King orders, or they just don't bother answering me at all. No one believes that I'm the Alpha King now.

I touch the pin on my collar. It's the only proof I have right now that the Council has transferred power to me. I didn't want to risk bringing the crown and sash to another kingdom in the middle of a war. But they'll have to pry this pin off my dead body.

I know there's more to being the Alpha King than the ceremony. Everything has transferred to me, including a more powerful Alpha voice. I just hope everyone sees who I am right away and listens to me.

There's nothing to fight about here. Our mate is going to unite the kingdoms, and we'll have a wonderful future. We'll open trade routes and improve our air travel. It'll be an economic boost to both sides as tourism starts, especially with so many people curious about what life is like in the other kingdom.

It makes me wonder why we've been kept apart for so long. I have a feeling it has something to do with the witch, but I have no idea what.

Finally, we reach a point where we have to stop and get out because all the other armies' vehicles are blocking the way. I see fighting up ahead, and I hear it, but it's hard to make out exactly what's happening.

We all pile out, and Trisha and her mother and sister join us.

"Rylee needs help," Trisha's sister says. "She's getting some children to safety." She looks at Trisha. "That's Ethan's mate. Are you coming, Trisha?"

Trisha shakes her head. "No, I think my place is here. Those are my people out there now. I'll be their Luna Queen soon."

"You're right," Rose says. "I'll go with Reeva and help Rylee. Please stop this madness, baby girl."

"I will, Mom."

They hug, and the other two women leave as Trisha stands bravely at our side. "Let's go," she says.

More than ever, I'm happy now that she has three mates because we protect her from three sides at least, which is better than one, as we move forward, dodging all the army vehicles to get to the heart of the fighting. When we get to the thick of it, I hesitate.

Trisha opens a mind-link channel with several people, and I soon realize it's her four fathers, her mother, her sister, and her brothers.

'My mate Damon is the Alpha King of these people now,' she explains. *'Please back off if you can, and he'll address them.'*

'Trisha?' One of the Alpha Kings sounds very excited to hear her voice.

'Rose? What are you doing down here?' another asks.

'Helping the people of our kingdom,' the Luna Queen replies. *'Now, do as our daughter says, and let the man talk to his own.'*

I can feel the violence taper off as all the Dark Forest warriors back away at their Alphas' command, and I move in. My warriors seem a little surprised that the enemies are backing off, so I make my way through them quickly, trying to find the commander. I don't know every warrior in our kingdom, but most can recognize me from the training college. Luckily, they all recognize me and at least don't attack.

I need to get to where they can all see me and the pin before I address the warriors. I jump up on a shipping container that has a good view of the battle and speak in my newfound Alpha King voice.

"My father is no longer Alpha King! I am your new king, and I order you to stop!" I hold onto the pin, which only the closest warriors can see, but I hope that's all I'll need.

Before I can say more, my mate jumps up and stands proudly beside me. "And I am his mate, your soon-to-be Luna Queen, Trisha

Forrest-Stone, princess of Dark Forest. I am mated by the Moon Goddess to three Alphas of Green Mountain, and together we will unite our kingdoms in peace!"

26

THE JOURNEY HOME

Trisha

I DON'T KNOW whether anyone is going to listen to me. They don't know me, so why should they? I just feel like these people need to know that they don't need to be afraid of Dark Forest anymore. And all the people here don't need to be afraid of Green Mountain.

Neither place is bad. They both have their problems, and there are some things that need work, but that's how life is. It's messy, and it's those imperfections that make a place unique. They give people opportunities to band together as citizens and make things better.

I look over the crowd of warriors in front of us. No one is saying a word, but they're not fighting, either. They haven't fought since Damon started talking, and they were dead silent as I said my peace. Damon wraps his fingers around my hand and squeezes, looking at me with pride in his eyes.

He turns back to the crowd. "I apologize for what my father has done," he says. "He was misled and guided by the effects of poison. A witch has been feeding him a poisonous plant for years. It was her influence that made him declare war."

Gasps ring out from throughout the crowd, and everyone erupts into whispers.

"But we're going to go back to Green Forest now," he continues. "We're going to return to our homes and spend our energy making things as good as we can. We're going to forge friendships with my mate's kingdom and create a new, better world for our pups."

He turns to my dads, brothers, my sister, and my mom, who are standing together close by. "And I apologize to the people of Dark Forest. These warriors were following orders from a madman, and his time as ruler is over. Though we'll have much to mourn about here, I hope that soon we can put our past behind us and move forward."

My dads and my mom all nod.

Damon turns to face the Green Mountain warriors again. "The first change is that we'll never again have one single ruler. There can be too many mistakes that way that could lead to the carnage we have here. Instead, my mate's other two mates, Braden Winten, Alpha Heir of Western Pine pack, and Alessandro Bianchi, Alpha Heir of Chestnut pack, will rule with me, the way the four Alpha Kings of Dark Forest rule with their Luna Queen."

There's more murmuring in the crowd, but I'm starting to see smiles.

"Let's go home and bury our dead, then we'll move forward." He nods toward the crowd with finality and steps down, putting both hands on my hips and lifting me down off the shipping container. I hug him and then my other two mates, and the crowd of warriors lift their fists in a cheer.

The energy in the crowd is electrifying, but it eventually dies down as everyone focuses on the task at hand. There are so many dead to recover that there's going to need to be a ship just for carrying them, and several warriors volunteer to staff it.

My dads organize the same effort for Dark Forest. Transport is arranged for the dead and injured, and Mom coordinates groups who will work on the cleanup.

"I think I should work on cleanup here," I say to my Alphas. "It just feels right."

"Of course, Trisha," Alessandro says. "Our people will work on the cleanup too. The faster we get all this done, the sooner we can move on."

Between dealing with the aftermath of battle and the complicated logistics of moving thousands of warriors back into ships for the trip back, it takes all night before everything is done. The first ships take off into the early sunrise as pink and orange rays cover the sky over the vast ocean.

I haven't slept at all since those few moments after making love to Damon, and I'm exhausted. Braden wraps his arms around me as my other Alphas step forward.

"We're all ready to go, Trisha," Damon says. He's explained to me that, rather than flying back to Green Mountain, the honorable thing to do is return with the warriors and the dead and injured, so we're going to go back by ship. "Are you ready?"

My mother runs up. "Oh, no. My baby girl—I'm not ready." Her eyes are already pouring out tears.

"Mom." I choke on the next words as Braden lets go of me, and I move in to hold her tight. I feel her tears on my cheek and know that mine are staining her dress.

My father, Tristan, puts his arm around Mom and gently pulls us apart. "Little flower, our Trisha has three strong Alphas to protect her. She'll always be safe, the way Mark, Eli, Reece, and I protect you." He looks at Damon. "I'm holding you to that agreement to get more flights into Green Mountain, and I promise, we will visit often."

"I wouldn't have it any other way," Damon says, shaking his hand.

My Alphas step back and give me a few moments with my family. My father puts his hands on both my shoulders like he always used to do when I was little. "Our little mini flower, how you've grown," he says. "I remember so clearly the day you were born. Nothing was more beautiful than you and your mother. Now, you're a grown woman, and soon you'll probably have a family of your own. I'm so proud of you for what you've become."

"Thanks, Dad," is all I can say.

One by one, my other three dads come up and give me tight hugs and words of wisdom. My father keeps holding Mom, who hasn't stopped crying.

Ethan steps up. "I'd like you to meet my mate, Rylee."

"Oh, my, you're stunning," I say. "Welcome to the family, Rylee. I'm so happy to have a new sister."

"And I'm happy to meet you," she says. "Your brother has said so much about you. I have one sister already. Now, suddenly, I have two more."

We laugh and chat for a few moments, then Matthew walks up. "Well, I don't have a mate to introduce, but I hope that happens soon. I'm glad you're happy, sis. They'd better take good care of you."

He gives my Alphas a little glare, and I have to laugh. "They will."

I give him a hug, and the last person to say goodbye is Reeva, who has about ten tissues in her hands and all of them are soaked.

"I don't want you to go," she says. "But I know you have to." She looks at my Alphas. "You did good, sis."

I giggle. "Thanks." I hug her, and she cries a bit more, but she dries the tears off quickly, and Reece, her father, steps up to put his arm around her.

I face my mother again, and I can finally say a few words without choking up. "I love you, Mom. You're the best. I owe you everything I am and everything I have."

"My baby." She hugs me again but then pulls back. "I love you, Trisha, my baby girl."

With that, I turn and head toward my Alphas. Damon and Braden take my hands, and Alessandro leads the way onto the boat that will take us to the ship. I turn around one more time and wave at my family, and they all wave back.

My Alphas help me onto the boat, and I keep my eyes on my family as we pull away from the docks, until they're too small to see, and we pull between some of the larger ships.

There's a ladder leading up to the massive ship that's at least twice as big as the one I first traveled to Green Mountain on. I wipe away the last of my tears as my Alphas make sure I get on board.

"Are you hungry?" Damon asks.

I nod. "Starving. I'm exhausted and emotional and ready to eat and then go to bed. So, who has dibs on me?"

All three of my Alphas start laughing.

"See? I told you she wouldn't mind joking about that," Braden says.

"Oh, boy. You've been talking about that?" I ask. I can feel the red creeping up onto my cheeks, though I have to admit, it's a huge turn-on to know that my three handsome Alphas have been talking about how they're going to take turns sleeping with me.

"Honestly, whoever gets me tonight—or this morning rather—might be a bit disappointed. I'm probably going to just collapse," I added.

"That would suit me just fine," Braden says. "I don't think you should sleep alone on this huge ship, and I'm happy to collapse with you."

"That's fine with me," Alessandro says.

Damon just nods, knowing he'll have to wait until it's his turn again.

"Let's go get food first," I suggest, and everyone laughs.

For a ship, this one has some great food, or at least, everything tastes wonderful, maybe just because of all the stress of the past twenty-four hours. I have a huge stack of buttermilk pancakes with three different syrups, one of which is apple cinnamon, and even a few strawberries on top, which makes me smile. I haven't told the guys yet what their scents are like to me, so they aren't in on my little joke. I'll tell them later.

Now, I'm truly exhausted, and I have a full belly. Braden takes my hand and walks me to our room, and I feel like I might even fall asleep on the walk, and he'll have to carry me. But I make it there, and the room is spacious and warm with a huge bed that looks like the most beautiful thing in the world to me right now. Well, except for the man beside me.

He puts his hand on my cheek and gives me a gentle kiss that he then deepens. I love kissing my Alphas. Braden tastes so good, sweeter than his scent even.

He chuckles. "I'd love to do this right now, but we're not going to. You're going to get some rest."

I'm too tired to argue so I just nod. He scoops me up, which makes me giggle, and carries me over to the bed, laying me down right in the middle of it. He undresses me, and it feels so good, but I can't enjoy it much right now except for how good it feels when he's finally naked next to me, cradling me in his arms as I drift off to sleep.

MY OTHER TWO MATES

Trisha

IT'S amazing to wake up with Braden's strong arms around me.

"Hey," he says.

"Hey." I look around and can't tell the time from the small amount of daylight I see in the small, high windows. "How long did I sleep?"

"Most of the day, but that's okay," he says. "We have plenty of time on the ship before we get home. Might as well get your rest. Plus, you needed to rest up for this." He wiggles his eyebrows, and I have to laugh.

He wipes a stray strand of hair away from my face and kisses me. I close my eyes, completely relaxing and enjoying the feel of it. It's much better than earlier when I struggled to keep my eyes open.

"Mm, I could do that all day," I say.

"Nothing stopping you."

I giggle against his lips but only for a moment since they taste so good. I briefly think about how I didn't get to have much time to relax with Damon, but I realize that I need to give all my attention right now to Braden alone. Besides, we'll have weeks aboard this ship with nothing much to do besides be together.

The idea sounds wonderful.

He pulls back for a moment and looks at me. He has the most stunning green eyes. The color is deep, like a gemstone. Our gaze is intense, like time has stopped a little while we just... connect. We're both still completely naked, and the feeling of his skin against mine gives me a warm feeling in my core.

I feel his rock-hard cock against my thigh, and I expect him to slide it in. But he doesn't. Instead, he kisses my warm skin, starting at my neck and trailing down, lingering at my breasts and sucking on my nipples, biting them lightly, which gives me pleasant chills.

I'm getting more antsy between the legs. I've only done it once before, but I know how good it feels when my mate is inside me. It's almost like my wolf is whining inside from the teasing.

"Patience, beautiful," he says, reading my mind.

I let out a little frustrated groan that makes him chuckle, but he doesn't speed up the process of kissing every inch of my body. I lie back and try to relax, knowing he's in charge, which somehow makes me even more excited. I need this man–now–but he's making me wait.

Finally, he reaches my inner thigh and nudges my legs apart, which doesn't take much because I'm happy to spread them wide. But he doesn't come back up. Instead, he keeps up the kisses, moving closer and closer to my pussy, but not quite touching it.

Then he starts to use his tongue, and something in me shoots off like a rocket. It's only been a couple of seconds, but the way he slides it around in all the right spots makes me quiver. I realize I'm coming, which I'd never known was possible with what he's doing, but then again, I've never done any of this before, so what do I know?

It's awfully fun to learn as I go along.

"Mm, so wet," he says with a moan. "You taste so good."

After a while, he kisses back up my body, gives me another look with those intense eyes, and slides inside me easily, I guess because of my orgasm.

He was right to go slow. The teasing and the coming beforehand has me in another world. He thrusts fast and hard, so much so that it's hard to find his rhythm but finally I do, and I scream out his name so many times it's probably echoing through the hallways.

I guess I'll have to be embarrassed about that later.

I can tell he's holding off for as long as he can, but in a few minutes, I feel him stiffen, and the way that feels inside me throws me into another orgasm. We both reach our peak together, and I don't even care how much noise I make as I go over the top.

I'm almost as exhausted as I was earlier by the time we're finished. We just lay there for a while, trying to catch our breath.

I giggle once we've calmed down. "I can't believe I screamed that loud on a ship full of sailors."

He chuckles. "Well, if they say a word about it, they have three Alphas to deal with."

I laugh, holding him tighter.

Neither of us wants to get up, but we're both hungry. We missed both lunch and dinner by now, so I hope the cook is understanding and will let us make something quick.

It turns out that he'll have none of that, kicking us out of his kitchen and insisting that he will prepare something for us. My other Alphas are waiting for us in the dining room, which is otherwise empty since the official dinnertime is over.

"Good evening," Alessandro says.

"Hi. I'm sorry I slept so long."

Braden pulls out my chair, and I smile at what a gentleman he is. It's funny. Not long ago I would have snapped at that kind of a thing and complained that he was coddling me. But I'm an adult now. Whatever issues I had with overprotectiveness from my dads and brothers flew out the window when I officially felt the mate pull. As far as I'm concerned, these guys can save me all day long.

"You needed your rest," Damon says. "We'll be on this ship for weeks, so there's plenty of time to get caught up on sleep and back on schedule. But now that we're all here, I'd like to talk about the logistics of how things will be when we get back to Green Mountain. I meant what I said about all of us ruling equally, so all three of us will be Alpha Kings while Trisha is our Luna Queen. So, we have to decide whether we keep our individual packs separate or combine them." He goes on to explain to me that his pack, Westmont pack, comprises the area surrounding the castle.

"I think our packs have a certain identity that we don't want to lose," Alessandro says. "I'll have to talk to my father since he's still technically in charge of Chestnut pack, but I don't think he'll mind passing it directly to my Beta when he's ready to retire."

"Same here," Braden agrees. "Once my dad retires, Andrew is more than capable of leading Western Pine pack. I think we should keep that separate from ruling the kingdom overall."

"That's perfect then," Damon says. He looks at me. "We're too far away to mind-link the Council, but I don't think they'll have a problem with a triple marriage."

"You mean I'll marry all three of you?" I ask. Until now, I haven't thought about how that will work.

"Well, if you want to, I mean," he says.

"It would be nice to have a proposal first." I laugh.

"Will you marry me?" they all ask at once.

I nod as we all keep laughing. It's unconventional, but so is having three Alphas for mates. "Yes," I say as soon as I can catch a breath. They all stand and come over to kiss me, one by one, each one lingering for a few minutes. It's the first time I've kissed Alessandro, and the spark of electricity makes me excited for our first night together.

"We need to finalize things, but since we're Moon Goddess-given mates, I don't think they'd object," Damon explains."

The cook brings our late dinner, and I thank him for his trouble. It looks delicious, a beautifully cooked bacon-wrapped steak with roasted vegetables on the side and mashed potatoes. I have a feeling Alessandro and Damon have already eaten, but they have no trouble downing their plates. I guess it takes a lot to feed an Alpha with all those muscles.

And I sure love all those muscles.

We talk more about the logistics of ruling together, though we can't finalize anything until we arrive at the Green Mountain castle. We also talk about sharing nights with me. I can't decide yet whether I want them to switch out every night or whether I'd rather have each one spend a few days with me.

"We have time," Damon says. "Let's just play it by ear for now. Later, we can talk about this again."

"Since Alessandro hasn't had time with you yet, I think his turn should be tonight," Braden adds.

I nod. I can't wait to make love to Alessandro.

We finish our meals and head up to the deck for some fresh air. The scent of the sea is strong, but I can still smell the wonderfully sweet apples and strawberries that surround me. I'm glad that's the mate scent of all three of my Alphas because that's my favorite.

I suppose that's how it works.

After watching the sunset together, Alessandro takes my hand, and I know I'll get to spend time with another of my Alphas. We walk together down the hallways toward his room.

He laughs. "The last time we were on a ship together, you looked like you wanted to beat me up like you'd done to that Randy asshole."

I giggle. "Well, you were scary then. How was I supposed to know you were my mate?" We walk for a bit, then I think of something and stop. "Did you know you were my mate then?"

"I suspected, as we all did," he says. "None of us really felt the mate pull completely until we rescued you from that dungeon. But you knew before that."

"I turned twenty-one that night," I explain. "But it was still strange to me that I had three mates, and I didn't say anything right away. Then, they kidnapped me."

"I wonder where that witch is now," he says.

I shrug. "I don't know, but I hope she's a million miles away."

We reach the room, and he unlocks it, pushing the door in to open it, then I feel his arms around me as he sweeps me up and carries me in.

When I recover from the surprise we kiss, my arm around his neck and feet dangling in the air as he closes the door with his foot.

28

THE THIRD MATE

Trisha

I USE my free hand to lock the door as Alessandro carries me into his room. I don't feel as nervous as I did with Damon or even Braden, maybe because I'm starting to get used to making love to my mates.

And I really like it.

I guess two times doesn't make me an expert, but it gives me enough experience to know that all my mates care about me and want to make me feel good. Damon and Braden were both so wonderful, and I know Alessandro will be too.

He carries me over to the bed and sets me right in the center of it, keeping my head lifted with one arm while he fluffs the pillow with another. He gently lets my head down, and I sink halfway in.

"Comfortable?" he asks.

I nod.

"Good," he says.

Then he walks away.

What?

I frown, watching him take a shopping bag out of a drawer. He turns around and comes back to me with a sexy smirk.

"What's that?" I ask.

"You'll see in a bit," he says, laying the sack on the nightstand.

Wondering what he's up to, I give him a sideways glance, but he just laughs and caresses my cheek with his palm, crawling onto the bed with me and moving in for a kiss.

He tastes wonderful, and just like the others, he smells of apples and strawberries, yet there's a different note in there—cinnamon, I think it is—that makes him unique. I close my eyes and relax to heighten the sensation, until I hear the plastic bag crumbling.

I open my eyes, but he puts his hand up to block that side of the bed. "No peeking. It's a surprise."

I giggle and close them again, happy to play along. Everything has been so serious up until now—the boy I needed to help, the kidnapping, Damon's father, the war—so much so that I'm ready for a little silliness.

And Alessandro is happy to oblige, apparently.

We kiss a while longer, and I feel his hands reaching up the bottom of my shirt, tugging at it, so I help him out and pull it over my head, throwing it and my bra onto the floor. I'm not self-conscious about being naked anymore, not with one of my mates. I know I can trust them, that I can always feel secure around them. In fact, I like the way they look at my body with a mix of lust and love in their eyes.

Seconds later, I feel him undoing my pants, so once again, I help him along, lifting my hips so he can slide them down. I open my eyes and look at him. His silver irises are stunning, actually the color of the precious metal, not gray, shimmering in the dim light.

"Close your eyes again," he whispers.

I obey, excited for his surprise and completely trusting that it's going to be wonderful. Then I feel something soft, tickling, running against my thigh. I can't help but open my eyes, and I see he's holding a bright pink, fluffy feather and running it along my skin.

I laugh. "Where did you get that?"

He laughs with me. "I bought it at a shop on the docks. A lady came back to check on her shop while we were all busy getting the warriors loaded for the ride home. She was really nice, and I felt bad that the battle had cost her business, so I wanted to buy something from her. I saw this and thought it was perfect. It's the end of a pen, see?"

He shows me the pen portion, which he's detached so he can rub me with the feather part on the lid, and I laugh again.

"Well, it's a beautiful feather," I say. "That's my surprise?"

"Not exactly." He leans in again and kisses me.

I moan lightly. It feels so good, I want more of this surprise.

He interrupts our kiss, and I pout for a second as he lifts himself up, but when I see why, I accept the few seconds of separation. He pulls his shirt off, first revealing his washboard abs and then his thick, defined chest muscles and the bulk of his strong biceps.

I appreciate the view, and I show it with a smile. All my Alphas are well-built and sexy, but just like their scents, there are subtle differences in their muscle tone. Alessandro is built like a bodybuilder, with bulk and definition. Braden has more of a runner's physique, though his muscles are still bigger than your average runner. Damon's body is somewhere in between, like an overall athlete who excels at everything.

All of them are beautiful.

Alessandro slips off his pants and boxers quickly and joins me back in the bed. The warmth is welcomed, though I would have enjoyed just looking at him a while longer. It's okay though. I'll have the rest of my life to appreciate his body.

As big as his arm muscles are, it's amazing how gentle his touch is. I imagine it takes a lot of restraint not to hurt me, but with him, it's effortless. I feel the bulk of his stiff cock against my leg. It's hard to believe that will fit inside me, but I know it will, and my need for him grows.

"You are gorgeous," he whispers, kissing my body as he travels down to my breasts, then lingering there, sucking and licking them. I feel every touch deep in my core, awakening the need for him, and now that I know how that's going to feel, I want to grab his cock and slide it in myself.

But I hold off, letting him take the lead, rubbing his strong hands against me and still tickling me lightly elsewhere. It makes me giggle, but the contrast between strong and light touch also adds more tingles of anticipation up and down my body.

Finally, it seems he's done with the teasing as well. We've waited a long time to be together.

He slides on top of me, holding up his massive, muscular body with his strong arms, and he slides his cock in. I expect him to go slow, but he doesn't, pushing in gently but not stopping until he's deep inside.

I quiver at the sensation of my body stretching to accommodate him.

"Baby," he moans, and his voice sends me shooting off into ecstasy. The effect on him is instant as he picks up the pace, and I meet his hips, my hands reaching down to grasp him and pull him closer. He moves harder, faster, and I explode into another orgasm, or maybe I never stopped the first one. I don't know and it doesn't matter.

How he can keep holding back I have no idea, but I know I'm not going to. I feel tingling from the tip of my head to my toes, his scent becoming somehow stronger and even more distinct.

"Mm, you like this, baby?" he asks, his voice gravelly and his breath labored.

"Yes." Just that one word sends him over the edge. I can feel my body stretching slightly as he stiffens more, and in the next moment, I feel him come inside me, the warm, wonderful juices moving even deeper inside me.

He slows his rhythm but doesn't quite stop yet, as though he wants to prolong the feeling for every possible millisecond.

So do I.

But after a while, we're both spent, and I imagine he can't keep himself supported up like that any longer after such an explosive orgasm.

He lies beside me, pulling me close and tucking my head into his chest, where I happily relax to the sound of his calming heartbeat.

Then I feel the feather tickling my butt.

I laugh. "Let me see that thing."

He gives it to me, and I run my finger along it. It's fairly long and sort of like those boa scarves they use in dances. I'm not sure how anyone would use this as a pen.

"What kind of a shop was that?" I ask.

He shrugs. "I have no idea. She had paintings and things for sale, candy, little trinkets."

"And you bought a feather pen?"

"Exactly."

I laugh and pull him in for a kiss. He still tastes fantastic.

We cuddle for a long time, talking about Green Mountain and what it's going to be like to live there. This has all happened so fast. One minute, I was sneaking out of the castle through the secret passages, and the next, I am engaged to three Alphas.

"I can't wait for our wedding," I say.

"Me neither," he agrees. "I can only imagine how I'm going to feel watching you walk down that aisle in your beautiful dress. Which one of us gets to rip it off you?"

I laugh. "None of you! It's my mother's dress. Reeva gets to wear it too and then our daughters, when it's their turn."

"I hope we have lots of daughters," he muses.

"You just like the idea of fighting off a bunch of boyfriends."

"Guilty," he says with a laugh.

"The poor girls," I say. "They're going to be terrified introducing the boys they're interested in to three dads. Let me tell you, it's not easy being a girl with multiple Alphas as fathers."

"I guess you would know that best," he says. "I don't want to be a mean dad, though. I want my daughters to feel right coming to me whenever they need something."

"It would be impossible for you to be mean," I say. "And my dads were never mean either, not one bit. It was just… overwhelming to have so many fathers always keeping an eye on everything I did."

"I can imagine."

"But I wouldn't trade it for the world," I add, smiling at my loving, wonderful mate.

2 9

HOME IN GREEN MOUNTAIN

Weeks Later
Damon

WE ALL STAND on the deck as we approach the Green Mountain docks. It's quite a sight to take in the hundreds of vessels in anchorage offshore so they can take turns at the docks. Ours has priority with the Alpha King and soon-to-be other Alpha Kings and Luna Queen aboard, so we head straight in.

I can see as we disembark that the castle has sent the royal escort, and thankfully the main car is large enough for all four of us.

"It's strange, being on land after being at sea for so long," Trisha muses. "I felt this last time. I think I'd rather fly for my visits, if that's all right."

I chuckle. "The Luna Queen can travel any way she wants."

"It's going to take me a long time to get used to that title," she says.

"It'll feel like second nature sooner than you think," I add.

We climb into the SUV and the driver heads toward the castle. It's good to see the familiar scenery pass by, and I'm happy to be able to experience it with my mate, especially now that the weight of war is off my shoulders, though we still have a reckoning with the families who have lost loved ones in the battle.

My main concern is how my father is doing. I link with Daniel as soon as I'm in range and this time, I remember to include Trisha from the start, as well as the other Alphas. "How is he doing?" I ask.

"Oh, good. You're home," he says. "He's awake sometimes, and when he is, he's distraught. Damon, he's starting to come back, and it's hitting him what he's done."

"I'll be there soon," I say. "Please get the Council together for a meeting as soon as possible."

I close the link as Trisha squeezes my hand. "We'll get him through it," she says.

Alessandro speaks up. "We'll convince him that it wasn't his fault. He had no way of knowing he was being poisoned."

"He had it rough when your mother died," Braden adds. "It was probably easier to trick him if that herb the witch used helped him forget."

"I'm guessing it did," I say.

"Damon, I didn't know your mother had passed away," Trisha says. "I'm so sorry. So much has happened that I haven't had time to ask anything about any of your families."

"Thanks," I say, giving her a light kiss. "It was very hard on me at the time. I was a teenager. My father pretty much checked out. I guess that's why I never thought twice about a strange 'healer' showing up. I figured she was treating him for depression and the loss of his mate."

"It's not your fault either, Damon," Trisha says. "You were hurting as well at the time."

I nod, though it's hard to really agree. I guess it's going to take some time to forgive myself as well. I have a beautiful, smart, kind, loving mate now though, and that gives me so much to be thankful for. I know she'll be the one to help me heal from all that.

But right now, my focus is on securing our future. The Council is waiting in the receiving hall when we arrive, and we all go straight there.

"Alpha King." The chairman bows his head, and the others follow suit.

"I need your counsel," I say without wasting any time. "This woman, the princess of Dark Forest, will be my Luna Queen. My friends are also her Moon Goddess-given mates. I need to know the protocol for such a marriage."

Elder Aerona, the only woman on the Council and a highly respected member of my cabinet, speaks. "Polyandry was once quite common among royals before the split."

"The split?" Trisha asks.

"That is the time when Green Mountain split from Dark Forest," Aerona explains. "It's been a few generations now, but then, the Luna Queen had two mates. Each loved her in their own way, but unfortunately, they loved power more. Travel was slow then. The journey was too long for her to go back and forth, and eventually, she chose to remain with the Alpha King of Dark Forest. Our king severed all ties, halted all improvement projects, and forbade anyone to ever go there again. He died with no heir, and the Barlowes stepped up."

"Oh," Trisha says. "Well, that makes sense then. We're told in Dark Forest that the old king went mad when his mate died of a broken heart. He ruled harshly because of it. That family ruled until my dads took over. King Gene was the last of them, though his parents were really nice. Maybe the mean part skipped a generation."

"Thank you for telling us that," Aerona says. "With the disconnect, we never knew what happened." She looks at me. "But it's clear that polyandry is legal and acceptable for royals, so long as the mates are true."

"We definitely are," Alessandro says quickly.

"All right," I say. "Well, we need to plan the ceremony. Trisha, we'll send messengers by plane to alert your family."

Her face lights up at the thought of seeing them again. I know we're going to have to take a lot of trips in the future. That should be easy with three of us to take turns going with her. I notice the bag she's holding and remember the statue.

"Oh, and I need a scholar who can tell me something about this." I motion to Trisha to hand me the bag, and I pull out the wolf statue. "This is the Luna Queen's personal possession, so it's only to be examined in her presence."

"I suggest having Reginald take a look," the Chairman says.

I nod. "Have him get in touch with me. Okay, I think all that's left is planning the wedding."

"I'd be happy to perform the ceremony," Aerona says.

I nod, grateful. "That would be perfect, thank you. Please have the events coordinator contact me." I look at Trisha. "How soon do you want to get married?"

"However soon they can get this together." She smiles at me, then Alessandro and Braden. "I just want to get started on our future."

We head into the dining room and enjoy a great dinner before settling into the parlor to talk to the wedding planner, Briana.

She asks Trisha about her ideal wedding and takes notes as Trisha replies. "I can put all this together in a month, if that works for you."

"Wow, that's quick for a wedding," Trisha says. "But that would be incredible."

"I can have the dressmaker meet with you tomorrow." Briana made another note.

"Oh. I really need my mother's input, I think. And I'd like my sister here as well."

"We'll get them here as soon as we can," I say. "I'll send the messenger tonight and ask them to return with him." I look at Briana. "Schedule the dressmaker for the next day, please."

We talk about a few more things but decide to make most decisions when Trisha can have input from her mother, so I call the household coordinator to talk about logistics in the castle.

"Alpha Alessandro and Alpha Braden will need their own permanent suites in the castle," I say. "The Luna Queen will need her own private quarters as well." I figure that regardless of who stays with her each night, Trisha should decide whether she wants to stay in their room or her own. It's going to be a different kind of marriage, so there should be a place where it's just Trisha's things for those times when she just wants to be alone.

"For now, you can stay in the guest suites," I tell them.

"Actually…." Alessandro turns to Trisha. "I need to go see my pack and my parents to work out all the arrangements back there. I don't want to leave you, but since it's Damon's turn to be with you tonight, maybe this is the best opportunity to get that done."

"Same here," Braden says. "I've got some logistics to handle, plus I need some time with my parents. I really don't want to leave you either."

"It's okay," she assures them. "I'd love to meet your parents and see your packs, but we'll have lots of time for that. It's probably best for you to handle things like that so the people of your packs don't worry."

I stand aside while she kisses them both goodbye, and after they're gone, she takes my hand. "Let's go see your father now."

By the look in her eyes, I can tell she knows I've been stalling, and I'm not even sure why. But I nod and start heading toward my father's room where we find him in bed.

Myla, one of our healer's assistants, sits by his side reading a book. She closes it and stands when she sees me enter the room. "He wakes up now and again then goes back to sleep," she explains. "The poison has been exhausting for him, and the sleep is necessary for healing."

I walk up to him, afraid to make noise.

"Wake him," Myla says. "It'll do him good to see you."

"Father," I say. I wait for a response before touching his shoulder and repeating it.

"What?" He awakens a bit startled, but after a few moments, he seems to have his bearings. "Damon… my boy."

It's the same thing he said to me last time, and I'm afraid he's going to start asking me for candy again.

But he doesn't. "Damon, they've been telling me everything that happened. You stopped that stupid war I started?"

"Yes," I say. "Everything is fine now."

"But they said… they said we lost a lot of warriors," he says. "That's all my fault."

"Father… Dad. No, it's not your fault," I insist. "You were given poison for decades, and it was bound to affect you. We found the antidote, and that witch will never be allowed within a thousand miles of this castle again."

"Coraline," he says. "You know, she was a pretty young thing when I first met her. Maybe that's why this old fool bought into her lies. She dyed her hair purple and said she was going to be the world's greatest healer."

"It doesn't matter now," I say. "She's gone, and you're getting better, Dad."

"Changed her name too," he says, continuing as though I've never spoken. "It used to be just Cora. She really hated Dark Forest. I'd swear she was from there if I didn't know better."

He closes his eyes and goes back to sleep instantly. Myla says that's normal and promises to keep watching him, so I turn and take Trisha's hand, walking her back to my room.

I truly need to sleep in my mate's arms tonight.

30

ROYAL WEDDING OF DARK FOREST

Ethan

I CHUCKLE as I walk down the hallway. *'Where does she have you held captive this time?'*

There's a pleasant giggle in my mind as Rylee answers me in our link. *'I'm not a captive. I like spending time with your mother. She's such a nice lady. But right now, we're in the library. She's going through the family archives.'*

'Oh, Goddess. That could take all day. I'm in need of my bride-to-be.' Just being in the same castle with Rylee drives me crazy. All I want to do is spend all day in her arms. With nothing to focus on but the wedding, I don't have anything to think about, so it drives me crazy when she's too busy with the wedding planning or talking to the rogue colonies.

She giggles again. It feels pleasant in the mind-link, like a warm tingling. *'Well, then you're going to have to talk your mother into letting me go for a few minutes.'*

'A few minutes? I intend to take you over and over again all afternoon.'

'Then you're going to have to arrange for that.'

I smirk as I round the corner and head into the library where my mother is standing over a huge table with giant tomes and scrolls spread out across it. Rylee has a smirk on her face.

Mom looks up. "Ethan! It's about time you got here. I was showing your fiancée the Silver family history for your father and his Beach pack."

"I'd love to go visit there," Rylee says.

"You should, when you're back from your honeymoon," Mom says.

"Mom, can I have my fiancée back, please?" I ask.

She frowns. "Oh, phooey. I was going to show her some of the centerpieces I made for the wedding."

I laugh. "Mom, why are you making things? We have an army of events personnel to put all that together."

"Well, because I want to," she says, almost with a pout. "How often do I get to see my baby get married?"

"Probably four times," I say. "And two of those will be within the next couple of weeks."

Mom giggles. "That's true, but still, each one is going to be special to me."

"I'll come look at them tonight after dinner," Rylee suggests.

My mom has her excited glow back. "Wonderful! I can't wait."

I wrap my arm around my mate, and we say our goodbyes, heading straight back to our room.

MY FATHER ELI adjusts my tie as I get ready for the wedding ceremony. I'm wearing my full-dress military uniform, a tradition for a future Alpha King of Dark Forest. I can't wait to see Rylee's dress. She's been very secretive about it, as has my mother and sisters, but I guess that's what brides do. I can see the point because it'll be a surprise when I see her walk down the aisle later.

It's going to be the best moment of my life. Well, that and the moment when she's officially my wife.

"I think we're ready to head over," Dad says. "I'd give you some fatherly advice, but I think you're doing really well on your own."

I laugh. "Thanks, Dad."

All my dads walk over to the Moon Goddess Temple with me. My mom has gone absolutely mad with the decorations. She couldn't put anything inside the temple since it's sacred, but the path leading to it, as well as the outside, is just covered in banners, flowers, and streamers. I'd feel sorry for the crew that has to clean this all up except that I know my mom and the dads are giving them all huge bonuses.

I walk in the side door and take my place at the front next to my brother, who shakes my hand.

"You look ready for your big day," he says.

"More than ready." I look at the crowd in front of us and smile. "Do you see anyone out there who might be your mate?"

He shakes his head. "Nope, nothing. I guess I have to wait."

"Maybe your mate is in Green Mountain," says a voice from behind us.

We look over at my other groomsmen, the Alphas of the other kingdom. They're all getting married to Trisha next week, so we'll be flying over there for that. I've never been there before, and I'm looking forward to it. Rylee doesn't mind that we'll interrupt our honeymoon for it. In fact, we've incorporated it into the vacation. The Alphas set it up so we can have some time in a private bungalow along the coast over there.

"I guess anything is possible," Matthew says.

The music starts, and my mom is formally seated. She looks positively giddy, and it makes me smile. It's always been a priority of mine to make sure she is happy, though my dads do a great job of that themselves. I'm glad she's enjoying my wedding. She's talked endlessly over the past month about her wedding to my four dads, which happened a while after her Luna ceremony when we were young. I guess it was a lot of work to have four babies, so they waited to make it official.

The music changes, and my sisters walk in, followed by Rylee's sister Katherine and two of her friends, then her matron of honor,

Rylee's best friend Amla. I inhale and let it out slowly as the music changes again and I prepare to see my beautiful mate. I know she is going to leave me breathless.

She doesn't disappoint. I don't know what that dress is made of, but she looks so graceful, like she's floating down the aisle with trails of white flowers and lace stretching out at least twenty feet. The dress fits every beautiful curve of her down to her waist, then it flows out in a wide skirt that tapers into the train. Her jet-black hair flows around her face in ringlets and waves, with tiny flowers sprinkled through her curls. What stands out the most is her eyes. Even before she gets close, I can see the deep blue orbs with flecks of silver in them. I'll never get tired of gazing into those eyes.

I'm only faintly aware of Isaac standing next to her, escorting her in the absence of her father, who like her mother, is deceased. He gives me the ceremonial handshake as he places my hand in Rylee's and then walks away.

I smile at my beautiful bride, and her silver flecks twinkle in the light.

The High Priestess begins the ceremony. "We are gathered here today to join our future Alpha King with his future Luna Queen. Chosen by the Moon Goddess herself, let no one come between the gift of the mate bond."

She continues with several elaborate prayers and chants, ones I've been hearing all my life, and I tune out, to be honest, while I just enjoy a few minutes of looking into those beautiful eyes. But then suddenly, it's my turn to speak. I turn toward her and hold both of her hands.

"Rylee, my beautiful mate, I've waited my whole life for you. I promise you my love forever, my unwavering protection, my undying respect. You will always be my equal partner as the woman who competes my soul."

The High Priestess nods toward Rylee.

"Ethan, my loving mate," she begins, "I never imagined a life with a mate. When I found you, my life changed, and I've never been happier. I promise you my forever love, my undying respect, and all the best of me. I'll always strive to serve our people as one. You are a part of me forever."

"Prince Ethan Forrest-Silver," the High Priestess says, "do you take this woman, Rylee Elizabeth Coleman, to be your wife and forever mate?"

It's the easiest question I've ever been asked. "I do."

The High Priestess looks at Rylee. "Do you, Rylee Elizabeth Coleman, take this man, Prince Ethan Forrest-Silver, to be your husband and forever mate?"

"I do," Rylee says with a wide smile.

"By the powers given me by the Moon Goddess, who blesses your union through her choice of you as natural mates, I pronounce you husband and wife. Prince Ethan, you may kiss your bride."

"Gladly," I whisper as I put my arms around her and pull her close, crushing my lips to hers and closing my eyes to feel every second of it. Reluctantly, I pull back since we're in front of such a huge crowd, and I take her hand in mine and raise our arms to the audience as everyone erupts in happy howls and cheers.

As we start down the aisle, I look at my mother, who is smiling with tears pouring down her cheeks. I stop, and Rylee lets go and motions toward my mom. I take a moment to give Mom a one-armed hug before going back to my wife and wrapping my arm around her as we go back up the aisle.

The events coordinator ushers us into a private room where we have a moment to ourselves. I kiss my wife again, this time deeper, letting our tongues play, breathing in her scent and basking in her taste, which is like the most delicious candy in the world.

She giggles against my mouth as she pulls back. "We have a few moments, husband, but I don't think we have time to make love yet with the entire kingdom out there waiting for us and, most importantly, your mother."

I laugh. "Well, a guy can dream, right?"

"You won't have time to dream because I'm not letting you sleep at all for the next forty-eight hours," she says teasingly.

"You're not doing a very good job of cooling me off," I say.

She laughs. "I wish we could be alone just as much as you do, but we have a responsibility to those who will be our citizens one day."

"That may be sooner than you think," I say. "I spoke to my dads earlier, and they are all thinking of retiring very soon. Matthew hasn't found his mate yet, but they may not wait for that. They'd like to have fewer responsibilities and more time with Mom."

"Well, that would be all right with me, if they're sure that's what they want," she says. "I hope Matthew finds his mate soon."

"I'm sure he will," I say. "Well, we'd better get out there."

She smiles, but I steal one more kiss from her before we step outside for the reception.

31

HONEYMOON IN PARADISE

Ethan

WAKING up to my wife is incredible, her soft body cradled in mine, feeling her heartbeat against my chest. She stirs, lifting her head up and looking around.

"What time is it?" Rylee asks.

"Probably time to get up," I say. "But I don't want to."

She chuckles, running her fingers down my cheek and bringing her lips to mine. I moan, tightening my arms around her to bring her closer. I pull back just enough to groan. "If you keep that up, we're definitely not getting up."

"Well, I'd better stop then because we're going to be late." She pulls back farther, tapping her finger on my nose with a giggle and scooting off the bed. "I don't want to miss a minute of our honeymoon on the beach."

I laugh, nodding and pushing myself up, knowing we'll have plenty of time for this once we get to the beach resort.

"I wish we could meet more people in your home pack while we're there," she says while getting dressed. "It sounds like this place is pretty secluded. I know everyone in Raven pack, but since it split off from Beach pack so long ago, I probably don't know anyone."

"Probably not, but we'll do that another time." I wrap my arms around her from the back and kiss her neck as she brushes her hair. "Secluded is what I want right now."

She laughs. "Me, too, but still, someday we'll have to take another trip there."

"We will."

We both make ourselves presentable for breakfast, the last official meal of the wedding event. Mom had insisted that the whole family stick around for it, even though Trisha and her Alphas need to get back to prepare for her own wedding. Mom and Reeva are going with them, and I'm happy they'll be there for her. The rest of the family will take a flight there the day before the wedding, and Rylee and I will leave straight from the beach resort via my pack's airport.

"I love this," Mom says, her eyes sparkling as she looks at us all around the table. Two of our dads sit on each side of her. For the rest of the table, one side is entirely taken by Trisha and her Alphas, while Reeva, Matthew, Rylee, and I almost cover the other side. If Reeva ends up having multiple mates, we're going to need a bigger table.

My father Eli stands. "I'd like to make a toast."

Everyone grabs their glasses.

"To our ever-increasing family," he begins. "I couldn't be happier that Trisha and Ethan have found their mates, and I know the other dads and your mother are just as happy. Congratulations again, Rylee and Ethan. Trisha, Damon, Braden, and Alessandro, we're all excited for your wedding next week."

"Here, here!" Tristan says. I don't think I've ever seen him so giddy. He loves all of us equally, I know, but I can tell how thrilled he is about Trisha's wedding.

We all stand, clink glasses together, then sit again as the servants bring out the feast. And it's definitely a feast. As usual, Mom has gone all-out, with every type of breakfast food you can imagine being brought out on tray after tray.

"Mom, there aren't that many of us," Trisha says.

Braden shakes his head. "I know I'm not complaining."

We all chuckle and start digging in.

After breakfast, it's time for Rylee and me to leave. Our bags are already packed and loaded into the car for the drive there. Thankfully, it's not too long of a drive to the private beach resort from here, though it's a couple of hundred miles west of the mountain resort where Isaac's pack is located.

We wave as I drive off, and Mom is crying again.

"I don't know how that woman has any more liquid in her for tears," I say.

Rylee laughs. "Aw, it's sweet. She loves you so much, and the rest of her kids too."

"She's always been the best mom. Hey, but when you hang out with her, don't listen to any embarrassing stories about me as a kid." I sneak a sideways glance at her. "It's all lies."

"Too late," she says. "She's told me all about you running around in diapers with your favorite floral blankie."

I turn my head back to watch the road. "Good Goddess."

Rylee just laughs.

We arrive at the beach resort, and it's even better than I remember it. I know they've been doing a lot of renovations, and they've assigned us one of the newest cottages. I inhale the fresh ocean air as we step out of the car, and I take her hand.

"Oh, my Goddess. It's beautiful."

I smile at her wide-eyed expression. She's always been in the mountains, never near the ocean before, where the water is so clear and blue it blends into the sky. We walk out on the private dock to our cabin as seabirds take flight.

"The bungalow looks like it's floating, the dock is so close to the water," she says. "And look, a beach!"

Located on a shelf that protects it from large waves, my pack has built a series of thatched-roof bungalows out in the water with built-up private beaches for each one.

She turns to me with a smile that lights up her eyes. "This is the most beautiful place I've ever been."

"And you're the most beautiful woman I've ever seen." I take her chin with my fingers and guide her mouth to mine, crushing our lips together as I feel her arms reach up to lock around my neck. I keep my eyes open, and so does she, so I look into her deep blue irises with their remarkable flecks of silver that sparkle in the bright sunlight.

A cool ocean gust sends her jet-black hair dancing in the breeze, and I brush it away from her face as we deepen the kiss. We pull back for a moment. I can tell she wants to go down the steps to the man-made beach below, so we do.

"The sand looks so soft." She kicks off her shoes, so I join her, taking her hand as we walk out into the warm water a few feet. "And the water is so warm."

I nod. "It's the perfect location here."

She turns toward the ocean, and I can't stop looking at her. Every move she makes is so graceful. Her slender arms reach up and pull back her hair, looping it around into a bun that she fastens with a hair stick from her pocket. Her skirt dances in the breeze while she plays in the water with her foot, holding onto me for balance. Her flawless caramel skin shines in the sun, and I can't help but run my hand over her shoulder and down her back, thankful that her dress is backless.

She looks up at me, and we kiss again. I gently coax her down until we're sitting on the beach. It's completely secluded since all the beaches are designed as private alcoves just off each dock.

"I'm going to make love to my wife on the beach," I say in a husky voice.

Her eyes fill with lust. "Oh? What a lucky wife you have."

"Not half as lucky as I am."

She giggles as I lay her back and roll us slightly so I'm on top of her, our feet completely in the water and half-buried in the warm sand. I kiss her again, running my hand over her soft, warm skin, gathering up her skirt and guiding my fingers up her thigh, my cock stiffening the closer I get to her heavenly pussy.

When I reach it, I get a surprise—no panties block my entrance. She wiggles her brows when she sees my face.

"You are a goddess," I whisper.

She's already completely wet, and I play with her entrance with my fingers for a few moments, teasing her by circling all the way around it when I know she wants me inside. I lift her skirt so I can appreciate all her glory in the afternoon sun. She spreads her legs wide and smiles up at me.

Goddess is an understatement.

My cock is so hard it's pulsating, but I still want to take my time to make sure she gets the most out of it. I move one finger in, slowly, watching her eyes as I go deeper. The smirk on her face melts into an expression of ecstasy, and I smile, pulling her dress away from her left breast with my free hand and wrapping my lips around her nipple.

I suck and pull on it, nibbling slightly before releasing it as I push my finger deeper inside her. That elicits a moan from her, and I smile and try it again, this time adding another finger to the mix, gently stretching her drenched pussy.

Her moans are louder now and her eyes are fully closed, her hand pulling the back of my head closer as I suck harder on her nipple.

I come up for air and tease away the cloth covering her other breast, giving it the same attention as I start stroking in and out with my two fingers. I don't know how much longer I can do this, but the look on her face is more than worth the effort to hold myself back.

But soon, I can't stand it. I climb up and unzip my shorts before I thrust my cock in. It slides so smoothly into her tight pussy that I almost come upon entrance, but again I hold back so I can pump in and out of her, watching her perfect breasts bounce up and down. I wrap one hand around both of hers and bring her arms over her head and into the warm sand, her cries getting louder as I pump deeper and faster.

Finally, I feel her clench around my cock as she lets go, and I happily release as the jolt of electric passion blurs my vision.

After a few minutes to catch our breath, she lifts her dress over her head and throws it onto the beach, stepping down into the small pool created next to the man-made beach. I strip down the rest of the way and join her, wrapping my arms around her and kissing her deeply, hugging her close to bring her naked body to mine under the water.

We spend four days and nights in the bungalow, never seeing another soul since the discreet resort personnel bring our food to our back door on the dock each time I order through the mind-link. We cuddle together in bed every night, the curtains swaying in the breeze as we watch the colorful sunsets.

Neither of us want to leave, but Trisha's wedding is soon, and we have to make our plane on time.

We'll have more fun later at the Green Mountain beach resort.

3 2

MATED TO THREE ALPHAS

One Week Later…
  Trisha

I THINK my mother could fly over the moon right now, she's so happy. It started with Ethan's wedding and hasn't stopped since. Now, she has tears pouring down her cheeks faster than the makeup artists can wipe them and fix her smeared blush. Luckily, these people in Green Mountain have a practically magic brand of mascara that won't run no matter how hard she cries.

That's going to come in handy for me, too, since her crying is just bringing out all the emotion in me. I can't believe I'm marrying my three Alphas today. Until my mom explained how her wedding worked and the High Priestess here had a meeting with me, I had no idea where I was supposed to stand or what I was supposed to do.

Things are a little different here in Green Mountain, but only by small details. After all, a long time ago, these two kingdoms were pretty much joined together.

I look in the mirror, and it seems like I'm staring at someone else. My hair is covered in a cascade of flowers and ribbons, my makeup is professionally done, and I'm wearing my mom's wedding dress, tweaked a little bit for me so it's a little more form-fitting around the hips. I look like a different person. Mom told me when she gave the dress to me that I could make whatever changes I want, so long as she got to see her "baby girl" in her dress.

I've come a long way since I snuck out of the castle every weekend night, and it hasn't even been that long, not really. My world changed when I met my Alphas and turned twenty-one, but I suppose that's what happens to every woman who goes through this in life. I never thought it would happen to me, but boy, did the Moon Goddess ever have a plan for me under Her sleeve.

"Mom, please stop crying," I say. My mom's poor makeup artists look like they're about ready to give up.

"I can't help it," she says. "One day, I hope you'll know how this feels, because having a child is the most beautiful experience in the world. They're so tiny. You hold them in your arms, and their little eyes look up at you. But then you blink, and they're teenagers, and not long after that, they find their own mates and start a life all their own. The day I had you, my four babies, was the most important day of my life."

"Well, I hope I have that day soon, too," I say. "Oh, and I had an exam with the healer this morning. She says I have two uterine horns. I guess that means I can get pregnant easier."

A waterfall falls out of my mom's eyes, and I send the makeup artists a sympathetic gaze.

"You do?" she says. "That's wonderful! I had two as well! I guess the Moon Goddess has all this planned after all. Oh, we should have your sister examined."

"Um, no," Reeva says from behind her. "I'll go ahead and leave my future a surprise, if you don't mind."

I laugh. "Yes, Mom. Let's not get ahead of things."

Mom looked a little disappointed, but not much since she was currently examining every inch of my dress and moving material around that didn't seem to be laying right.

"Well, we'll know one day," she says in defeat.

"I wonder why our brothers only have one mate each," Rylee says from her seat across the room. "Well, Ethan anyway. I guess we don't know about Matthew yet."

Mom shrugs. "Hard to say. I guess it's just a thing for the Forrest women."

"Oh, great," Reeva says.

Mom just ignores that, and I laugh. My sister always has her nose buried in a book, and I don't think she's given much thought to who her mate will be.

I look at Rylee in the mirror, and she's positively glowing. She and Ethan have taken two days off their honeymoon to switch kingdoms, attend my wedding, then they'll go off to a beach resort along the south coast of Green Mountain. Damon has shown me pictures of the place his people booked for them, and it looks gorgeous.

The events coordinator pops her head in, her arm wrapped around a clipboard with a huge stack of papers. "We're ready to begin if you are," she says.

I nod, and Mom starts crying again.

"Mom, you can't keep crying," I say. "You have to go out and get seated so I can get married."

She frowns and wipes her eyes as the makeup artists move in again. I guess everyone will expect the mother of the bride to cry, so no one is going to mind if she's got smudges of foundation and blush all over her cheeks. She's always beautiful, no matter what.

"All right, ladies, let's head out," Reeva says. She's my maid of honor, and she's wearing a beautiful emerald gown, the royal color of Green Mountain.

Everyone piles out except Mom, who insists on hugging me again, but at least she's careful not to mess up my hair. I toyed with the idea of having it in an up-do, but my long, curly locks are my signature look, so I've gone with leaving it down with the floral decoration.

My dads come in and peel Mom off me. The logistics of a wedding with four dads, not to mention the three Alphas I'm marrying, are a bit complicated. We've decided to have Mark and Eli walk Mom to her seat, then have Reece escort his daughter Reeva, even though the maid of honor usually walks by herself. It just seemed like the right thing to do before Reece sits down with Mom in the front row. My father Tristan will walk me down the aisle.

Everyone leaves to take their places but him, and I take a few breaths, my nerves finally kicking in.

He chuckles. "You'll do great, baby girl. I'm so proud of you."

"Well, you are now, but you were pretty pissed when I snuck out and sailed halfway across the world," I joke.

"Yep, and if I would have known where you were, I would have come after you," he says. "But I'm glad I didn't. You already had three protectors waiting for you here. We will, however, discuss that kidnapping a bit more one day."

I nod and laugh, not answering that.

"Are you ready?" he asks.

I nod again. "Yes. Let's go."

I take his arm, and he leads me to the temple which is a bit of a walk from the room where I was getting ready. Luckily, the weather is cooperating, and my hair isn't blowing all over the place.

I hitch a breath when I walk through the breezeway and see all the people outside the castle cheering when they see me. I give them a wave, and they cheer louder. The temple here is huge, but not big enough to hold everyone in the kingdom who wants to see the wedding. I guess it's not every day their Alpha Kings get married.

Braden and Alessandro had their coronations a few weeks ago, so they're officially Alpha Kings. Once I'm their wife, I'll also be the Luna Queen, which will be part of this ceremony.

I hear the cue as the music changes, and Dad walks me forward.

My three Alphas are all standing on the right, their eyes gleaming. I can't take my eyes off them, though my sister and brothers are on the other side to stand up for me.

Damon, Alessandro, and Braden all smile as I get closer, and once we're there, Dad shakes hands with all three of them.

"Take care of my baby girl," I hear him say.

"Yes, sir," they all answer.

The High Priestess starts the ceremony with a long chant and multiple prayers to the Moon Goddess for the protection of the kingdom, Alpha Kings, and Luna Queen. There aren't any real vows to say, which I'm thankful for. That would be too confusing, and I'm promising my love equally to all of them. All I'll need to do is affirm three times that I want to be their wife.

But their part comes first.

"Alpha King Damon Barlowe, do you take Princess Trisha Forrest-Stone as your lawfully wedded wife and Luna?" the High Priestess asked.

"Yes, I do," Damon said, smiling.

"Alpha King Alessandro Bianchi, do you also take Princess Trisha Forrest-Stone as your lawfully wedded wife and Luna?"

"I do," he says. His eyes twinkle as he looks at me.

The High Priestess turns to Braden. "Alpha King Braden Winten, do you also take Princess Trisha Forrest-Stone as your lawfully wedded wife and Luna?"

"I definitely do," Braden says. He winks at me and wiggles an eyebrow, and I want to chuckle.

The High Priestess doesn't look very amused, but she turns to me and keeps going. "Princess Trisha Forrest-Stone, I'll ask one at a time whether you accept the role of wife and Luna to the three Alpha Kings. First, Alpha King Damon Barlowe?"

"Yes, I do," I say. I can't stop smiling.

"Alpha King Alessandro Bianchi?"

"Yes, I do." I feel thumping in my heart.

"Alpha King Braden Winten?"

"Yes, I do." I feel moisture welling up in my eyes, and I try to hold it back.

The High Priestess continues. "Now, do you pledge to be an honorable Luna Queen to the people of Green Mountain? Do you accept the task of caring for all the people, particularly the young and the female, and agree to put your heart and soul into every decision for their welfare?"

"Yes, I do," I say.

She does a few more prayers and chants, then I bow my head as she places the crown on my head. She turns to my Alphas and says, "She is now your Luna and mate, through the love and mercy of the Moon Goddess."

I can't help but let the tears fall as they all come forward and wrap their arms around me one by one, sealing our love with a kiss. I'm now the wife and mate of these three wonderful Alphas, and the new Luna Queen of my new home, Green Mountain.

I see my mother cry as I walk back down the aisle with my husbands.

<hr>

I'M EXHAUSTED from all the dancing. Not only have I had dances with all my husbands, but I've also gone through all my dads, my brothers, and a few uncles and Betas as well. We walk over to the punch bowl to give me a break.

"The food is incredible," Braden says. "I'm glad your mom brought over the catering staff from Dark Forest so we could try some of their traditional wedding dishes."

"I couldn't have stopped her if I'd tried," I say. We all laugh, and I look around at the crowd, noticing my sister with her head in a book, or some sort of paper, and I wonder what it is.

"Can you guys give me a minute?" I say. "I need to talk to my sister."

"Of course," Damon says.

I kiss each of them one more time before heading over to the table and plopping down next to Reeva.

"What 'ya reading?" I ask.

She looks up, her eyes a little wide with surprise, before she laughs. "Oh, sorry. I was just reading this and didn't even see you come up."

"What is it?"

"A brochure for a university in Green Mountain," she explains. "They have an incredible history program there."

"You should totally go," I say.

"You think they'd let me?" she nods in our dads' direction.

"They can't very well say no," I say. "Their other daughter is the Luna Queen here. I think it would be fun for you. And history sounds right up your alley."

She nods. "Yeah, I'll think about it." She looks across the room. "You'd better get back to your gorgeous Alphas. They look like they need a little more Trisha."

I laugh with her and stand, but I stop for a minute while she gets a strange expression on her face. "What's wrong?" I ask.

"Oh, nothing," she says. "I just felt something weird. It's gone now. I guess it's nothing."

"Okay. Let me know if you need anything."

"I will," she says.

She goes back to her brochure, and I head back to my husbands who are talking to someone. He leaves before I get there and walks outside.

"Who was that?" I ask.

"Just a professor at our university," Braden says. "So, how's our wife and Luna Queen liking her wedding reception?"

I smile. "It's perfect, and so are all of you."

I couldn't ask for a better life than one with my three Alphas, and I just can't wait for the future.

ALSO BY BELLA MOONDRAGON

The Alpha King's Breeder series:

Bought by the Alpha: The Alpha King's Breeder Book 1

Loved by the Alpha: The Alpha King's Breeder Book 2

Lost by the Alpha: The Alpha King's Breeder Book 3

Luna of the Alpha: The Alpha King's Breeder Book 4

Legacy of the Alpha: The Alpha Kings's Breeder Book 5

Daughter of the Alpha: The Alpha King's Breeder Book 6

Descendants of the Alpha: The Alpha King's Breeder Book 7

Shadow of the Alpha: The Alpha King's Breeder Book 8

Son of the Alpha: The Alpha King's Breeder Book 9

The Luna's Vampire Prince series:

The Culling

The Kingdom

The Conquered

Pregnant With Four Alphas' Babies

Chosen As the Breeder

Mated to Four Alphas

Threats Against the Breeder

At War for the Breeder

The Stolen Breeder

Four Alphas, Four Babies

Becoming the Luna Queen

Descendants of the Breeder

Desired by the Devil series

Whispers of the Devil

Banter of the Devil

The Mafia Kings series

Indebted to the Mafia King

<u>Loved by the Mafia King</u>

Claimed by the Mafia King (releases 11/15/2024)

Sign up for Bella's newsletter here.

Follow Bella on Facebook here.

www.ingramcontent.com/pod-product-compliance
Lightning Source LLC
Chambersburg PA
CBHW070420310726

48977CB00003B/776